TURN OF THE TIDE

Recent Titles by Elisabeth McNeill from Severn House

THE EYEMOUTH DISASTER STORIES

THE STORM
TURN OF THE TIDE

THE EDINBURGH MYSTERIES

HOT NEWS
PRESS RELATIONS

A BOMBAY AFFAIR
THE SEND-OFF
THE GOLDEN DAYS
UNFORGETTABLE
THE LAST COCKTAIL PARTY

DUSTY LETTERS
MONEY TROUBLES
TURN BACK TIME

TURN OF THE TIDE

Elisabeth McNeill

This first world edition published in Great Britain 2006 by
SEVERN HOUSE PUBLISHERS LTD of
9–15 High Street, Sutton, Surrey SM1 1DF.
This first world edition published in the USA 2007 by
SEVERN HOUSE PUBLISHERS INC of
595 Madison Avenue, New York, N.Y. 10022.

British Library Cataloguing in Publication Data

McNeill, Elisabeth
    Turn of the tide
    1.   Widows - England - London - Fiction
    2.   New business enterprises - England - London - Fiction
    3.   Disaster victims - Scotland - Eyemouth - Fiction
    4.   Eyemouth (Scotland) - Social conditions - 19th century - Fiction
    5.   Domestic fiction
    I.   Title
    823.9'14 [F]

    ISBN-13: 978-0-7278-6456-7

Except where actual historical events and characters are being
described for the storyline of this novel, all situations in this
publication are fictitious and any resemblance to living persons
is purely coincidental.

All Severn House titles are printed on acid-free paper.

Typeset by Palimpsest Book Production Ltd.,
Grangemouth, Stirlingshire, Scotland.
Printed and bound in Great Britain by
MPG Books Ltd., Bodmin, Cornwall.

To little Lola

Introduction

Turn of the Tide tells what happened to some of the women and children whose lives were devastated on Black Friday: 14 October 1881.

The previous book, *The Storm*, tells the true story of how, on that day, half of the fishing fleet of the Scottish Borders town of Eyemouth was sunk in a freak storm, and 121 of the town's men drowned.

Many of them died within sight of their homes, frantically clinging to the Hurkar Rocks that jut up from the water just outside the harbour mouth, and their deaths were witnessed by wailing women on the quay.

No family in the small town was unaffected by the tragedy, which left behind 80 widows and 260 orphaned children, as well as several fatherless unborn children. People who had been prosperous and contented became grieving paupers overnight.

Contemporary newspaper reports of the dreadful storm aroused a wave of sympathy from people all over the country, and money poured in to help the afflicted families. Within two weeks, the vast sum of £50,000 was contributed by rich and poor alike – including contributions from Queen Victoria, who sent £100, and a railway signalman who sent half a crown.

This generous response proved to be a problem, however, for the town authorities could not agree on how and to whom to distribute so much money – the equivalent of more than a million pounds today. In the end, an Inspector of the Poor called Steven Anderson was brought from Edinburgh to

1

supervise the handing out of the charity money on behalf of a committee of local worthies. Anderson was a poor choice because he was a weak-willed, avaricious man who could not resist peculating on his own behalf from such a princely sum.

Though the money was enough to set the town back on its feet by buying new fishing boats to replace the twenty-one that had been lost, the official committee, consisting mainly of bigoted churchmen, decided instead to give miserly weekly handouts to deserving women and children. Children were to receive half a crown a week till the age of fourteen, and widows five shillings each, providing they led moral lives. Yet these families had enjoyed at least seven pounds a week when their men were working, and they also had their own codes of conduct and morals of which churchmen disapproved. For example, few women married before they became pregnant, many marriages were 'irregular', and wives never took their husbands' surnames.

Among the recipients of this 'thin gruel' charity were three loosely related women, Effie, Rosabelle and Jessie, who clung desperately together, forming a new family unit for themselves. Effie, the oldest, lost her husband and three sons; her beautiful daughter-in-law Rosabelle lost her husband of one week; and pert Jessie was about to be married to Effie's second son Henry, who also died. Both Rosabelle and Jessie were pregnant.

The Storm tells how they, like the other women of the tragic town, tried to adjust to their changed circumstances and make new lives for themselves. They all went through the stages of grief – sorrow, followed by anger and finally by a kind of resignation. Effie found solace in caring for her sons' women and their posthumous children, especially Rosabelle's son Aaron, whose mother could not clear her mind of the conviction that his father had been a sort of sacrifice for his birth. She found it hard to love him and would have exchanged him for his dead father, if she had been given the choice.

Jessie, the third of the trio, was the first to recover her spirits and will to survive. Shortly after Rosabelle had Aaron, Jessie gave birth to a girl called Henrietta and, though Effie originally had doubts about her suitability as a wife for her son, she proved to be a loving mother and a support for them all.

Jessie set about finding work, not only for herself, but for her brothers and sisters too, because her father and brother had also died in the storm and her distracted mother descended into alcoholism and quickly died.

Rosabelle was a different matter. To Effie's disquiet, her gloom and sorrow deepened as time passed. Her father was also drowned in the storm and her mother, who could not come to terms with her loss, committed suicide by throwing herself off the pier in Berwick-upon-Tweed.

Effie feared that desolate Rosabelle might also try to kill herself, for her state of mind never lifted – in fact it worsened when Steven Anderson, the distributor of the fund money, developed a passion for her. Though he had made an advantageous marriage to the daughter of a rich Eyemouth shopkeeper, he was obsessed by Rosabelle's beauty and persistently stalked her, much to her terror.

Because the girl was a skilled seamstress, Effie persuaded her to take a dressmaker's job in nearby Berwick-upon-Tweed, partly to get her out of Eyemouth during the day, but Anderson continued to lay in wait for her at night, and finally cornered her in the dark and would have raped her had she not been able to knock him out and escape.

Next morning his dead body was found floating in the dock.

Convinced she had caused his death and could be hanged for her crime, Rosabelle reacted hysterically and Effie feared she would attract attention from the police and give herself away, though there was no reason to believe she had actually murdered Anderson. Jessie took charge and bundled Rosabelle off to London in the company of a mysterious woman, one of her Berwick customers who had seen her talent with the needle and invited her to help set up a dress-maker's business in the capital.

After the train carried Rosabelle down to England, Jessie and Effie stayed on in Eyemouth with the children, uncertain if they would ever see her again, especially after Willie Wake, a demented old man who wandered the quay at night, let slip to them that Anderson had been hit on the head and pushed into the dock. Though he did not name the murderer, they were afraid he would implicate Rosabelle and so they resigned themselves to losing her for ever.

Turn of the Tide tells the story of what happened to the three women and their children in the difficult years ahead . . .

One

O n the day after Rosabelle arrived in London, Steven Anderson was buried. The funeral cortège was one of the most impressive the town had ever seen. His wife Hester would have no less.

The silver-handled coffin was borne solemnly downhill from Beechwood in a huge ebony-coloured hearse with engraved glass windows and drawn by four black horses with towering plumes on their heads. Their harness was covered with black velvet and they bent their necks, mouthing silver bits, as they paced along.

Effie and Jessie, each carrying a child, were among the crowd of bystanders who watched the procession go by. Since Rosabelle's departure Effie had not left the house and going to watch the funeral was almost a relief.

'They've put on an awfy grand show for him,' whispered Jessie.

'I always think the more relieved a woman is to be rid of a man, the more show of mourning she puts on. Maybe Miss Hester is glad to be shot of him,' Effie replied.

'I don't know about her, but her father certainly is,' was Jessie's reply.

'How do you know?'

'By watching and listening.'

Hester passed by in the first mourners' carriage. She looked the picture of grief, encased in total black with a tear-soaked handkerchief held up to her face. Her father beside her was ill at ease because she refused to address a word to him.

Her brother Everard was in the second carriage, along with two dejected-looking women – Anderson's mother and sister, who Hester had refused to allow into the first carriage. They were terrified of her.

After the mourners filed into the church, people in the crowd began chatting among themselves, airing various theories about Anderson's death. The most popular opinion was that he had done away with himself because he'd been caught peculating the disaster fund. Others were kinder and thought he might have fallen into the harbour by accident, but there was also a vociferous faction who liked the idea that he'd been murdered, but why or by whom they had no idea. One thing was certain, everyone agreed: Miss Hester would not rest till she found out the truth.

Effie shivered inwardly when she heard this and turned to Jessie to say, 'The wind's snell. The bairns might catch cold. Let's go home.'

As they hurried along the alley that led to her house they came upon Willie Wake sitting on the ground with his back against the wall. His lips were blue with cold and he was shivering like a beaten dog.

Effie bent down to him and said, 'Aw Willie. You shouldna sit oot here in the cauld. Come wi' me and I'll gie you a wee dram to warm you up.'

He staggered to his feet and held on to her shoulder, saying, 'Ye're a kind-hearted weman like yer mother and yer granny.'

In her house the fire was blazing and he sank into Jimmy Dip's chair before holding out his skinny hands to the heat. The fire brought out his rank smell, but he'd wakened their pity and Effie poured out a stiff drink for him, putting it carefully in his hand.

'Drink it up. You look as if you need it,' she said.

He downed it in one and held out the glass for another, which she indulgently provided because he was as pathetic as a child. The second whisky galvanized him and he sat up in the chair, suddenly animated.

'Thank you, Effie. Now I'll gie you a wee sang,' he said. She replied, 'All right, just a wee one I hope.'

'It's a sang I wrote myself,' he announced, standing up and rocking on his heels.

'Sing away,' laughed Jessie, who was always ready for a party, but the smile froze on her face when the old man started singing . . .

> The deil cam oot on a cold black night,
> And saw a man and lassie fight.
> The lass was fair wi' yellae hair
> 'Twas better if she wasnae there
> Cause he was oot to dae her wrang,
> But she was swift and she was strang.
> Ae big push was all it took
> Tae shove the bugger in the drook.
> The deil thoct him better die'd
> When he fell aff the auld pier heid.

The two women in the kitchen stared at each other in horror. For a moment Effie wondered if the old man was trying to blackmail them, but then realized he was expecting to be congratulated on his song. The drink had gone to his head, that was all. The awful thing was that he'd seen what had happened between Rosabelle and Anderson and now he was singing about it!

Jessie's reaction was more impulsive. Face flaming red, she ran up to Willie and shoved him so hard in the chest that he sat back in the chair with a thud.

'I dinna like that sang, Willie. Dinna sing it again,' she told him.

He looked up at her with rheumy eyes and said, 'Dinna worry, Jess, dinna worry. I'll haud my tongue.' As he made for the door neither of the women tried to stop him.

When the sound of his feet could no longer be heard on the cobbles, Jessie moaned, 'He knows. And he's as daft as a brush. Do you think he really will keep his mouth shut?'

7

Effie shook her head. 'We'll just have to hope. But one thing's for sure: Rosabelle winna be able to come back here as long as he's alive.'

Two

When Rosabelle set foot in London for the first time she was overwhelmed by the crowds. The enormous station where they arrived seemed to be crammed with men, women and children, all jostling and pushing at the same time. As her companion Rachelle propelled her through the throng, she shrank back in alarm and panic made her cringe like a wild animal emerging from the seclusion of a forest.

'I want to go home. I want to go back,' she said, but Rachelle gripped her arm firmly and pulled her towards a hansom cab. 'You'll get used to it. Get in.' She tapped the cabbie on the shoulder with her parasol and gave brisk directions. In a few minutes they were put down at a rooming house where they rented two furnished rooms.

'Where is this?' Rosabelle asked, looking around.

'Bloomsbury. But we won't stay long. I'll soon find something better,' said Rachelle cheerfully. Being in London seemed to have rejuvenated her.

Timidly Rosabelle lifted the edge of the heavy window curtain and stared down into a rain-washed street that was crowded with cabs, pedestrians, dogs, sharp-eyed little boys who looked like thieves and vagabonds, loitering women who occasionally stopped to talk to passing men, and ragged old tramps who searched the gutters – for what? she wondered.

'I'm not sure I'm going to like this place,' Rosabelle said, without turning her head.

Rachelle laughed. 'Give it a chance. Half an hour's not enough. At least here there aren't any sea views.' But her

9

voice softened as she added, 'New places can be frightening. Give me time to get my money sorted out, and we'll go into business. Before I left Berwick I had my palm read by a gypsy and she predicted fame, fortune and good friendship for me . . . You're the friend she had in mind, I think.'

This startled Rosabelle. As far as she was concerned, her only friend was Jessie. She was not sure that she even liked Rachelle.

'I don't believe in fortune-tellers,' she said shortly.

'I do. The same gypsy predicted that my lover would drown at sea – and she was right about that. I know another fortune-teller in Stepney and I'm going to ask her about setting up our business. Come with me and she'll read your hand too.'

Rosabelle shuddered. The last thing she wanted was to have her future told. What if another tragedy awaited her? She'd rather not know. 'Certainly not! It's stupid,' she said sharply.

Rachelle laughed, not at all offended. 'But at least come out with me now and see this wonderful city.'

'What time is it?' asked Rosabelle.

'Half past nine,' said Rachelle.

'It's too late. People in Eyemouth are sound asleep by this time.'

'And London's only coming to life. Put on that big cloak of yours and come out with me.'

'Are you going to the fortune-teller?'

'I might.'

'Then I'll stay here.'

Rosabelle spent her first night in the city sitting at the window until the first streaks of dawn appeared in the sky and she realized Rachelle had still not returned. Her heart began thumping in panic and she was convinced she had been abandoned, left in this heartless city with only her carpet bag and three half guineas stitched into the bodice of her chemise. Her consolation was to feel the hardness of the coins against her left breast.

She was about to put on her cloak and make her escape

when there was a tap at the door and a young girl appeared with a big jug of steaming water which she placed on a washstand.

She said something to Rosabelle, who stared in confusion, not understanding a word.

'You foreign?' the maid asked slowly and loudly. Rosabelle understood that at least.

Am I foreign? I suppose I am, she thought, and nodded.

'I'll tell mistress you want cawfee, awright?' said the girl and flounced out.

In minutes, a tray appeared with bread and a steaming jug of dark brown liquid like nothing Rosabelle had ever tasted before but which warmed and soothed her. She was still making plans to escape when she heard the sound of feet on the landing and Rachelle burst in.

'Good. You're up and dressed!' she cried as she helped herself to the dregs of the coffee pot. Her face was beaming as she spread a fan of banknotes out on the tabletop. 'I've had a very useful night,' she cried, throwing out a hand like a performer in a circus.

Rosabelle stared at the sheaf of notes in disbelief. 'What a lot of money!'

'Yes, it's enough to find us a place to rent in Mayfair. We're getting out of this poky hole as soon as possible.'

It was like being swept up in a whirlwind. Before she knew what was happening, Rosabelle was hurried out of the rooming house and into another cab that carried them along streets that became wider and smarter with every hundred yards they covered.

Today the sun was shining, and she stared out at elegant houses and grand shops as they passed. Seeing her amazement, Rachelle laughed and asked, 'Changing your mind about London yet?'

'Perhaps,' was the cautious reply.

'Wait. There's better places than this. We're going to Mayfair. I saw my gypsy last night, and she told me not to waste time.'

Rosabelle wondered if Rachelle was deranged. Perhaps she ought to head for the station and home. Would it not be safer to brave out the Anderson problem than career around London with a mad woman?

She could not leave, of course; she had no idea where she was, and anyway, part of her was intrigued.

Before midday they arrived at a flat-fronted, elegantly furnished eighteenth-century house off Piccadilly. Number 49 Half Moon Street.

To her amazement she heard Rachelle tell the landlord, 'I'll take it for five years.'

When they were alone again, Rosabelle protested, 'You've signed a lease for five years! What if we don't get any work?'

'Trust me. We will.'

Installed in Half Moon Street three days later, Rosabelle summoned up enough courage to walk down the street on her own, but was appalled at how little regard London people seemed to have for each other. No one stopped to chat, said 'good day' or smiled when they passed her. The carts and carriages flowing along Piccadilly looked like a terrifying wall, impossible to breach.

Because she wanted to cross to the other side, Rosabelle stood timidly among a group of women beside a street sweeper who stepped into the traffic and grandly stopped its flow so they could cross.

Shamefaced, she noticed that the other women tipped him for this service, but she had only her one and a half guineas in the world, and there was no way she was going to spend it on tips. She was still not convinced that Rachelle's plans would come to fruition.

Returning from her walk, she spotted Rachelle dismounting from a hansom cab at their front door. She was carrying a large parcel and the cabbie followed behind her with two more.

'Look at what I've got,' she cried, throwing her parcel on to a settle in the hall. The paper burst apart revealing a bolt of beautiful material, pale ivory in colour, patterned with a design of little flowers made out of silver wire and interspersed with scrolls of tiny jet beads.

'How lovely,' said Rosabelle, gently fingering a corner of the cloth and admiring the way the silver thread glinted in the sunlight that shone through the open front door.

'It's French,' said Rachelle.

'Like you,' laughed Rosabelle.

'And very expensive, like me too,' was the reply.

They held out a length of cloth between them and relished its beauty.

'What sort of dress would you make with it?' asked Rachelle eagerly.

Rosabelle frowned for a moment, then said, 'A ball gown . . . yes, a ball gown. With ivory silk rosettes on one shoulder and hooped into the skirt on the opposite side like this . . .' She caught hold of the edge of her own heavy serge skirt and pulled it up in a loop.

'Any sleeves?' asked Rachelle.

'No, just little shoulder caps, and a deep, rounded neckline.'

'Can you draw it for me?'

'But who is it for? Who will wear it?'

'A girl of eighteen, with dark hair, I'm told. She – or at least her mother – is looking for a rich husband. Make her a dress that will catch one.'

'But who is the girl? How did you meet her?'

'I haven't yet, but two days ago I put an advertisement in *The Times* with a post box address. I worded it to show that our work is expensive and exclusive and already I've had two replies. This material is for the first one.'

'What if the customer doesn't like my design? And stitching this cloth won't be easy because of all those metal threads,' she said.

Rachelle waved a casual hand. 'Don't worry about that. My outworkers will make it up. They can stitch anything. I didn't bring you to London to do stitching. You're too valuable for that. The first thing you must learn is to value yourself. The girl's mother is the wife of a rich brewer from Birmingham. If she doesn't like it, I'll make her think she's the one who's wrong. But before we go to see our clients you'll need some smarter clothes.'

Rosabelle recoiled, 'I couldn't go into those big shops . . . and anyway I've no money.' The half guineas were her secret cache.

'I'll buy you a dress, and while I'm out, start drawing that ball gown. Draw, draw, draw,' Rachelle said, disappearing through the door.

She came back an hour later with a flax-blue dress sprigged with small flowers and a little straw boater hat with a ribbon of the same blue. The dress had a tight bodice and long tight sleeves with drooping lace cuffs, and it made Rosabelle look girlish and virginal.

Rachelle clapped her hands and said, *'Très jeune fille.'*

I don't know what she means but she only speaks French when she's trying to bamboozle me,' Rosabelle realized.

By the next morning Rosabelle had finished her ball gown drawing, and Rachelle's reaction was outright admiration.

'Lovely. Perfect. You're a clever girl, even if you can't read or write!'

'I can sign my name,' protested Rosabelle, wishing she'd never revealed her secret.

'Sign this drawing then and we'll take it to our client. With a talent like yours, reading and writing doesn't matter – but who taught you to draw?'

'Nobody. I've always done it. I used to draw on wet sand with a stick when I was small, and in winter I scratched pictures on the hearthstone of the fire.'

'I was right, you're a real artist. Dress up in your new clothes and we'll take this design to Mrs Alfred Crutchley in Mount Street. And when you hear me telling her the price of the gown, do not gasp!'

A bleak-faced butler opened the door of the Mount Street house and ushered them into the morning room to await the lady of the house, who soon came rustling downstairs, as round as a barrel, with an enormous bosom and very broad shoulders. *If her daughter resembles her, my dress will look ridiculous*, thought Rosabelle.

No such doubts seemed to worry Rachelle, who became as French as Empress Eugénie, rolling her Rs and her eyes, as if to show that the English and their language was very inferior.

'*Bonjour madame, regardez!*' she said, advancing with the design and a material sample which she spread on top of a spindly table, contemptuously pushing aside a collection of little silver ornaments as she did so.

Intimidated already, Mrs Crutchley bent over the display and breathed, 'Oh my!'

Rachelle shot a triumphant glance at a white-faced Rosabelle.

'You like?' asked Rachelle, looking down her formidable nose.

'Oh yes! Such beautiful material.'

'And the drawing? You like that?'

'It's lovely.'

'You have good taste, madame,' said Rachelle, as if she was bestowing a sweet on a child.

'I'll send for my daughter,' said the lady, ringing for her butler, who was despatched with a summons. 'If Miss Alice is still in bed, she must get up at once,' the mother ordered.

To Rosabelle's relief the daughter did not much resemble her mother. She was small, slim, pert, pretty, and more self-possessed. She flounced in wearing a flowing silk peignoir in peach pink and matching satin slippers.

Her mother said coaxingly, 'Alice dear, look at this lovely design. These ladies can make it up for you to wear at Lady Stevenson's ball next week.'

Frowning, Alice bent over the design, and different expressions crossed the faces of the three women who looked on. Rosabelle looked scared; Rachelle haughty; and the mother anxious.

At last Alice said, 'It's nice. I like the rosettes. But what material will be used? I don't want satin.'

Rachelle stepped forward and presented the material sample. 'It's French. And the rosettes are silk.'

Again the fine cloth worked its magic. Alice held it up to the light and said, 'How beautiful. But won't it scratch when I'm wearing it?'

Rachelle made it sound as if Alice was stupid to ask that question. 'It will be fully lined, *naturellement*.'

'Do you like it, my dear?' asked Mrs Crutchley.

Alice nodded. 'Yes, I do.'

Her mother looked at Rachelle and said, 'The ball is next week. It's Alice's first in London. Are you sure the dress will be ready in time?'

Rachelle pouted. 'It is a work of art, madame, and works of art take time, as I'm sure you realize, but I can assure you it will be ready.'

It was obvious that Mrs Crutchley wanted that dress for her daughter more than she had ever wanted anything in her life.

'Measure her now,' she said.

Rachelle looked around as if she was estimating the value of the furniture in the room and was not impressed. 'Our fees are considerable, madame, because our clientele is very exclusive.'

The word 'exclusive' acted like a cattle prod on Mrs Crutchley. 'I am not looking for cheapness,' she said with dignity.

'To make this dress for your daughter, and deliver it within six days, I will charge ninety-five pounds.'

If Rosabelle had not been warned to hide her surprise, she would have gasped aloud at this effrontery. Even Alice paled a little.

'That's rather a lot,' said Mrs Crutchley weakly.

Rachelle gathered up the material and the design as if to leave. 'There will not be another dress like it in any ballroom in London. See how cleverly it is designed, in

16

sections, like a skin. Only the most skilled workers can do that—'

'I'll pay,' Mrs Crutchley interrupted. 'Please measure her now.'

An hour later, back on the streets of Mayfair, Rosabelle found her voice and asked, 'Will she actually pay us ninety-five pounds?'

'Of course she will. I won't hand it over till she does.'

'It's more than two years' wages for most people,' said Rosabelle, remembering the five shillings a week that was grudgingly dispensed to Eyemouth's widows.

'Perhaps for some people, but not for us. This is only a start. We'll make the dress, and make it well because if Alice catches a rich husband when she's wearing it, she'll be our customer for life. Come on. There's no time to waste,' cried Rachelle, gaily waving her parasol.

Back in their rooms they collected the full bolt of material, and when they set out again in a hansom, Rosabelle asked, 'Where are we going now?'

'To Whitechapel,' said Rachelle.

Rosabelle felt like she was entering another world, even more frightening than Bloomsbury. The dignified streets and big houses of Mayfair seemed a million miles away, and the squalor of Whitechapel's streets and alleys made even Eyemouth's fulzie heap, their local word for a pile of rotting fish guts, seem hygienic and pristine. Stinking rubbish was piled on every corner and people slunk around like alley rats, but Rachelle sat back in the cab, unfazed by the rubbish-littered streets and the tumbledown buildings crowded round filthy courtyards.

They descended from their cab at the mouth of a narrow alley hung around with washing lines. Unshaven men in doorways stared rudely at the smartly dressed strangers threading their way past rotting vegetables and stinking puddles. Slatternly women wandered drunkenly about with squalling children trailing behind them, and scrawny dogs fought in the gutters. There was an overwhelming smell of stale alcohol.

'Hey, you,' an old crone shouted at Rachelle, 'what d'ye want 'ere? Slumming or Gospel bashing?'

Rachelle spun round and glared at her. 'Get aht, back to your dog kennel, you old bitch!' she spat.

Her accent was no longer French, but pure Cockney, the same accent as cab drivers used to curse each other in the streets.

'Where are we going?' Rosabelle asked anxiously.

'Don't worry, I know my way around. This is where our seamstresses work.'

'Here?' Rosabelle thought of the lovely silver-shot material and feared it would be sullied in these sordid surroundings.

'They're poor but respectable,' was Rachelle's sharp reply.

The alley ended at a warehouse with a peeling wooden doorway which Rachelle pushed wide to reveal a large open space roofed over with glass and metal girders. At the far end women were bending over long cutting-out tables.

One looked up when the door creaked open and stepped away from the others, glaring suspiciously at Rachelle. Then with a laugh she said in obvious surprise, 'Blimey, look who's 'ere! Madame Fancy Pants 'erself.'

The others looked round and gasped too.

''Ello, Eth,' said Rachelle.

''Ello, Sadie, you're looking very fancy. What's brought you 'ere?' Eth had a hard, shrewd face and no front teeth. It was impossible to guess her age.

Rachelle laid her precious parcel on the table and said, 'Take a gander at this.'

Eth's manner softened as she appreciatively fingered the material. 'It's good stuff,' she said.

'It cost me plenty,' said Rachelle, producing the drawing. 'Can you make it into this in a week? The measurements are on the back.'

'It'll cost you.'

'Eight bob a day for three of you if you finish by Friday morning. We'll do the final fitting ourselves.'

'Make it ten. We'll have to line it, and what about those rosettes?'

'I'll get them. Nine bob and a tanner.'

Eth shook her head. 'Ten bob or nothing.'

'All right, but good work and no mistakes.'

'No mistakes.'

Rachelle was in a hurry to get away after she handed over the cloth. Taking Rosabelle by the arm, and without introducing her to Eth, she said, 'Come on. Let's get out of here.'

In another hansom on the way home Rachelle lit up one of her exotic-smelling cigarettes and said, 'I'll buy the silk rosettes but we'll keep them till we get the dress and you can put them on at the end. They'd only steal half of them.'

Rosabelle's head was swimming. Ten shillings a day for dressmakers working in what looked like a shed, with no sign of any refinement or luxury. 'You're sure they won't spoil it?' she asked anxiously.

Rachelle laughed. 'They make court dresses for peeresses in there. You can never tell what goes on behind closed doors in the East End, believe me.'

Five days later, a heartbreakingly beautiful ball gown was delivered to Mount Street, and fitted on to Alice by Rosabelle. The girl and her mother received it with rapture.

From her share of the profit, Rosabelle sent a £10 money order to Eyemouth.

A letter came quickly in return but, because Effie knew that reading was difficult for Rosabelle, the note was short and simple. Rachelle read it aloud.

'Thank you for the money. It is good of you to send so much. Aaron is well and growing fast. Jessie's girl too. Do not come back yet because people have not forgotten about the relief man and Willie Wake is talking out of turn. Love from Effie.'

'Who is the relief man?' Rachelle asked.

Rosabelle flushed. 'A man who gave out money to the widows and orphans of men lost in the big storm. He used to follow me about and I hated him.'

Rachelle shrugged. 'You can hardly blame him for that. You could have an army of followers if you wanted them.'

Rosabelle shuddered, remembering the night Anderson died. She wanted no more followers and was terrified by what Effie said about staying away from Eyemouth. She knew that was not written lightly.

She did not confide her feelings to Rachelle. Their relationship was friendly but still remote, and they shared no confidences, preferring to talk of business – especially as they wondered how Alice Crutchley's dress had been received at the ball.

Even Rachelle showed signs of anxiety about that, wringing her hands and groaning, 'Was Alice up to wearing a dress like that? Perhaps she was too common?'

Rosabelle sat silent. At least she still had her three half guineas.

On the seventh day of their suspense, a barouche rolled up at their door and two women got out. One was Mrs Crutchley and the other her equally rich friend, Mrs Arbuckle, who also had a daughter to be married. They swept into the salon and Mrs Crutchley announced, 'The ball gown was such a success! Dear Alice had three proposals in one night. One from a baronet!'

'Can I guess which one she'll accept?' said Rachelle wickedly.

Mrs Crutchley wanted Rachelle and Rosabelle to start work on her daughter's trousseau, and when they left, Rachelle pirouetted round the room, holding out her skirts with both hands. 'It's happened! The fortune-teller was right. Now we can engage salesgirls and print those business cards. We're on our way!'

Next day packets of cards arrived, proclaiming:

Rachelle and Rosabelle
Dressmakers to the Gentry and Ladies of Fashion
49 Half Moon Street, Mayfair

Rachelle hired three well spoken lady assistants to deal with the customers, and set Rosabelle up in the large first-floor studio where she was happy and absorbed. Meanwhile, beautifully dressed and made-up, Rachelle went out on the town, passing out business cards, making contacts and taking orders. For materials she visited silk weavers' workshops at Spitalfields, and riverside warehouses where cloth and ribbon importers stored their wares. Rosabelle went with her to select French ribbons in a dingy Wapping shed owned by a crippled man with clawlike arthritic hands. He handled his beautiful wares with exquisite delicacy and was obviously an old acquaintance of Rachelle's. When they left, Rosabelle asked, 'How do you know that man so well?'

'Remember Nisbet? He used to bring ribbons, cloth and lace in from France and that fellow was a customer. He only buys the best.'

The mention of the fisherman Nisbet, Rachelle's lover who was also drowned in the fishing disaster, brought back a rush of unwanted memories for Rosabelle. When she was busy she could keep the past in the back of her mind, but every now and again an unwanted thought, or the glimpse of a baby being pushed along in a basketwork perambulator by a uniformed nurse, would induce in her an unshakable feeling of guilt – and terror. But even if she wanted to go back, she knew she must not. Effie would let her know when it was safe.

Three

Jessie was going up in the world. When a woman who assisted at the cheese counter died suddenly, to the surprise of the other shop assistants, Mr Stanhope offered Jessie the job.

When she tied the long tapes of a white apron round her waist for the first time, she was filled with a feeling of pure delight. On the counter before her were mounds of cheese on the marble slab – white cheese, orange cheese, yellow cheese, cheese with blue streaks running through it like veins in a human body. She put a hand on the biggest one in admiration. Though she could not read the labels that were stuck on each sample, she was confident that it would not take her long to learn which was which, and she was right. Within a week, she knew them all, and could describe the differences in taste with devastating accuracy.

Only rarely did Reverend Cochrane spend money at Stanhope's but he was particularly partial to cheese. When he stepped up to the counter, he was surprised to be served by the twinkling-eyed girl he'd seen in the fishing town.

Jessie cheekily asked him, 'Oh aye, Mr Reverend sir, what do you fancy today?'

He blushed and said, 'Some cheese, please. What do you recommend?'

'This one fair nips your tongue, and that one melts away like butter. Or maybe you fancy the stinky one,' she said, indicating a sharp Cheddar, a French Brie and a ripe Gorgonzola.

He laughed and said, 'I'll have the one that melts.'

'How much do you want?'

'Only a small piece to accompany my supper . . .'

She laid out a sheet of greaseproof paper and cut off a large slice.

'Oh, that's too much,' he protested, thinking of the cost.

'Don't you worry. I'll only charge you for four ounces,' she told him with a wink and a devastating dimple. She liked the lanky minister because he was not holier-than-thou like some other clerics in the town. When he went out of the shop he felt he was walking on air. For the first time in his life, Alan Cochrane was in love.

'Have you heard about Jessie going to work in Stanhope's?' Effie asked her friend Euphen as they sat together in Effie's kitchen cuddling a baby each.

'Yes, she's going up in the world. I saw Mr Cochrane the minister in there buying cheese and staring at her as if she was a goddess. His maid told me he buys a bit of cheese nearly every day now . . .'

Effie laughed. 'Men can't resist Jessie and she can't resist them. It's aye been her trouble.'

Euphen sighed. 'She's lucky to have got back on her feet so soon.'

'It's not soon, it's two years since the storm. I don't expect Jessie to spend her whole life mourning. She knows that life goes on. She cannae greet for ever . . . It doesn't mean she didn't love Henry. She's making the best of things, and good luck to her.'

'She wouldn't have got into Stanhope's shop if Miss Hester wasn't laid up, though. That baby of hers must be due any day now,' said Euphen.

The two women nodded together. Hester, in an advanced state of pregnancy, would never parade herself in public in such a condition. It was not proper for someone in her class of society. She hadn't set foot in the shop for three months, and during that time Jessie had got her foot well and truly in the door.

'We'll see what happens when Hester comes back, but I think Jessie'll be all right. She's the sort that gets through,' said Effie.

'She's lucky to have you to look after Henrietta for her,' said Euphen.

Effie bent to kiss the baby girl. 'It's a pleasure to look after this wee soul – and Aaron too. Jessie comes and goes to suit herself. She's aye been the same. Fanny says she even disappeared during her wedding at Lamberton. One minute she was there, the next she wasn't. She was probably meeting some man. Trust Jessie!'

Euphen nodded. 'Aye, it was different with Rosabelle. I don't think she'll ever get over Dan. Have you heard from her?'

'She's a good lass. She sends money every week, and always more than we need, but the letters don't say much – just that she's well and busy making clothes for rich women in Mayfair – so she must be doing well.'

'My word, I've heard about Mayfair! But she's good to send money for Aaron. I was afraid that she didn't feel much for the wee lad. She was too broken-hearted about Dan,' said Euphen.

Effie agreed. 'Her heart was broken. She really wants to love Aaron, but something holds her back. Maybe it's because he looks like his father, poor wee soul. That pleases me, but it didn't please her. She doted on Dan. It takes some folk a lifetime to get over that kind of loss.'

'And she couldn't feed Aaron when she was so ill after his birth. Breastfeeding a bairn always makes a bond,' agreed Euphen.

'Your William's old enough to be getting married. You could have your own grandbairn to cuddle soon,' said Effie in an effort to cheer up her friend.

'If I'm able,' was the mumbled response.

Effie looked hard at Euphen. 'You're not well, are you? What's the matter?'

'I'm weary. I've never really picked up since Black Friday.

I was so sure Alex was dead. It was terrible. All my strength seemed to leave me and it hasn't come back to this day.'

Effie patted her friend's hand. 'You'll feel better soon,' she said.

While Effie and Euphen were talking about her across town, Hester Anderson felt her first birth pains and quickly went into full labour because her baby was more than a week overdue.

When her father walked home for his afternoon nap, he found his house in turmoil with Hester upstairs in the throes of giving birth, attended by Dr Wilkie and a local midwife. Her howls reverberated down the stairs and even into her father's library sanctum.

The labour lasted till five o'clock in the evening, when she gave birth to a healthy little girl who bawled lustily as she entered the world. When he realized that two different voices were shrieking together, the old man poured himself a whisky from a crystal decanter and drank it down in one.

He was sipping at a second when the doctor came downstairs to announce, 'It's a girl, eight pounds and a very good pair of lungs!'

'I know. I heard her yelling,' said the new grandfather, but he did not go upstairs because he knew Hester would not welcome him. She had not addressed a polite word to him since Anderson's funeral. Instead he scribbled a message to his son and sent a servant to the post office to telegraph it to Edinburgh.

Everard arrived later that night and took charge of the household, carrying messages between father and daughter.

'The baby is to be called Louisa and she's doing well. Hester's tired and weepy though,' he told his father.

The old man sighed. 'Does she want to see me?' he asked.

Everard shook his head. 'No, she's as intransigent as ever but she'll climb down in time, I hope. I'm sorry, Father.'

'Can you bring the baby down so I can at least see it?' was his father's next question.

'I'll try.'

Eventually a nursemaid descended the stairs with a blanket-wrapped bundle which she carried over to the old man by the library fire. With gentle fingers, he pulled the covers away from the tiny face and stared into it. Then he sat back and sighed.

'The living image of her father, unfortunately,' was his only comment.

He was right. Louisa Anderson had the same heavy jaw and bovine expression as Steven.

Next morning at the breakfast table, Robert said to his son, 'Tell Hester I'll hire a nurse for the baby, and when she's able to travel, I'll send them to the south of France for a holiday. I hear it's very pleasant there.'

Everard eyed his father. *He wants her out of the way and I don't blame him*, he thought, but only nodded and said, 'That's a good idea. In France she might meet someone else to marry. There's nobody suitable round here. She had her eye on Cochrane for a bit but he doesn't seem to be the marrying kind.'

'I agree with both of these statements,' said his father.

Because some women of her class stayed in bed for a month after giving birth, Hester kept out of sight for a time, but was too anxious to get out and about to languish for long.

The grocery was on her mind because she reckoned that when her father died it would be hers and she intended to keep a close eye on it. She had not been in the shop for four months and there was no knowing what the assistants were doing without her to chivvy them.

Two weeks after Louisa's birth, still dressed in her mourning clothes, she walked briskly down to the store.

Pausing proudly on the monogrammed doormat, she surveyed her kingdom, eyes as sharp as an avenging angel, looking out for signs of carelessness, slovenliness or mal-administration.

At first everything seemed perfect and she almost relaxed. Then she spotted the laundress Jessie behind the cheese counter, *wearing an assistant's white apron.*

The two women stared at each other and Hester's face darkened. 'Mrs Maltman, or whatever you're called, what do you think you're doing?' she thundered.

'Serving cheese, Miss Hester,' said Jessie innocently.

'You are a washerwoman. Take that apron off this instant and go home,' commanded Hester.

Jessie stood her ground, putting her fists on her hips and looking belligerent. The rest of the staff and a handful of customers stopped all transactions and watched with eager interest.

'Do – as – I – say,' said Hester slowly and loudly when she saw that the girl was rebelling.

At that moment Robert Stanhope emerged from his office and took his daughter by the arm. 'You are distraught, my dear. You should go home and rest,' he said.

'I am not distraught. What is that fishwife doing in our shop?' demanded Hester, pointing at Jessie, furious at being forced to speak directly to her father.

Robert was stronger than he looked. He grabbed her arm, nodded to a male assistant who jumped to the big front door and pulled it open so that Hester could be propelled through it.

Her father firmly shut the door behind her. Watched by an interested crowd, Hester walked away, but fury radiated from her like simmering heat.

Meanwhile, dusting his hands, her father went back to his office. Eyes dancing and on the verge of laughter, Jessie looked round at the spectators and asked, 'Anybody wanting cheese?'

At breakfast next morning in the house of Jessie's family, the Johnstons, Mary told her mother and siblings that she was getting married.

'Who to?' asked Jessie.

Elisabeth McNeill

Mary blushed. By far the most modest and retiring member
of her family, she'd been courted by a few lads but never
settled finally on anyone.

'His name's John Goodfellow and he's a fisherman from
South Shields. I met him on the quayside a couple of years
ago,' she said.

'When's the baby due?' Jessie asked.

Mary jumped angrily up from the table and set the dishes
rattling. 'I'm not having a baby – not yet.'

The others looked at her open-mouthed and Jessie laughed.
'That's a first for our family then,' she said.

A bleary-eyed Bella mumbled, 'I'm glad, lass. When's the
wedding?'

Mary said, 'In two months. We're trying to get a bit of
money together first.'

'Another first,' said Jessie.

'What about the laundry work?' asked Patrick, the oldest
of the boys and very money-conscious. In a few months he'd
be fourteen, and no longer eligible for his half crown a week
from the disaster fund.

Jessie looked at him kindly, for he was a favourite of hers.
'Don't worry, I'll find you a job,' she said.

'Not on a boat. I don't want to go to sea,' said Pat.

Their mother sighed into her teacup. 'Oh dear, Robert's
son and he doesnae want to go to sea . . .'

'He's got more sense,' snapped Jessie and turned to her
brother to tell him, 'I know the man who has the livery stable.
Would you like to learn to be a coachman?'

Pat's face lit up. He loved animals, especially horses. The
others round the table stared at Jessie, wondering how she
managed to arrange things the way she did.

After her family went their various ways for the day,
Bella yielded to temptation. For several days she'd been
sober, but the news of Mary's marriage gave her an
excuse to celebrate so she walked to the Ship Inn where
she put her relief money on the counter and demanded to
be served.

The landlord looked doubtful. 'Do your lassies know you're here?' he asked.

'Of course they do. I'm celebrating because Mary's getting married. I want to drink to her health. Jessie doesnae let me take a bottle into the house any more, but she'll no' stop me having a wee drink if I'm oot,' she said.

A nip of whisky was put up and swallowed in one gulp. Bella reeled, leaned heavily against the counter, and shoved the glass back asking for another, but the landlord shook his head.

'I canna. Drink's killing you, Bella.' He was right. Her body had swollen to a grotesque size, and her hands shook with continual tremors.

She had always been a troublesome drunk and this time she lived up to her reputation. 'My lassie's getting married and I want to toast her. Give me another!' she screamed, smashing the empty tumbler against the top of the bar.

Shards of glass flew in all directions and the landlord looked for assistance at a couple of young men sitting in a corner. They moved in. 'Come on, Bella, dinna make trouble,' they coaxed because they were sorry for Johnston's widow, another casualty of the storm.

She yelled insults and oaths, scratching at their faces with taloned hands, and screeching like a cat. They backed away. 'Gie her a drink, for God's sake. It might knock her out,' said one of them to the landlord.

'All right, but go and fetch her Jessie from Stanhope's while I'm putting it up,' was the host's reply.

When she heard that Jessie was to be summoned, Bella headed out of the door and collided with Euphen, who happened to be passing. She cried out in dismay when she saw her sister.

'You shouldn't be drinking at this time in the morning. You promised the girls you wouldn't. Come home with me,' she pleaded, grabbing Bella's arm.

Amazingly her entreaties were successful. Blearily the drunk woman leaned her head on Euphen's shoulder and started to weep. 'Oh, I'm finished. I'm done,' she groaned and allowed herself to be led away.

Halfway along the street Bella gave a groan, her knees buckled and she staggered, pulling her sister down with her. Euphen fought to keep them up, but Bella was heavy and she had little strength so they both collapsed in a heap on the cobbles.

Euphen was the first to recover. When she stood up, she saw that Bella was motionless. Kneeling down, she realized in a second that there was no point trying to raise her sister. She was dead.

People crowded round and men lifted the body to carry it home. When Jessie came running round the corner, still wearing her white apron, she saw her mother being toted along like a rolled-up carpet.

'Drunk again?' she asked angrily.

A weeping Euphen laid a hand on the girl's shoulder. 'No, not drunk. She's dead. I think she had an apoplectic fit.'

Jessie burst into tears.

The younger children arrived home from school to a house of mourning and found their mother laid out on the biggest bed. Following an old superstition, Euphen had draped cloths over all the mirrors.

A stern-faced and composed Jessie gathered the youngest children into her arms, trying to console their tears. Though Bella had been a careless parent, they all loved her and overlooked her failings.

'Oh, Jessie, I won't have to go into an orphanage, will I?' sobbed the baby, little Betsy.

'Don't worry, I'll look after you,' she was told.

Jessie found herself taking on responsibilities she would carry all her life.

Four

Although they had worked together for over two years, the relationship between Rachelle and Rosabelle was still remote. But they were very successful and, as their fame grew, they relied more and more on each other. Rachelle would be nobody without Rosabelle's dressmaking skills, and Rosabelle would never forge ahead without Rachelle to push her on.

Sometimes, as they talked business, they secretly looked at each other and wondered, 'What goes on inside your head?'

Rosabelle knew that Rachelle certainly was not French, but her background remained a mystery and she seemed to be able to adapt herself wherever she went, like a transparent fish that takes on the colour of any water in which it swims.

Rachelle was equally curious about whatever scared Rosabelle so much that she did not dare to go home even for a visit. She revealed the extent of her fear when a letter came from Eyemouth telling her the result of an inquest.

'They held an inquest on Anderson in Duns sheriff court and returned an open verdict,' Effie wrote.

When Rachelle read the letter out, Rosabelle's face blanched and she gasped. 'Open verdict. What does that mean?'

'That no one really knows what happened, I suppose, so it's been left open.'

'Open?' Rosabelle sounded as if she could hardly breathe.

'If they ever find out more they can enquire into the case again,' said Rachelle, eyeing the other girl curiously. 'Why are you so worried?'

'No reason, no reason. Curiosity.' But it was obviously more than that.

'Who died? Were you involved?' persisted Rachelle.

'Involved? Me? No, never! Never . . .' The vehemence told its own story. Rachelle shrugged. She had enough secrets of her own not to bother about anyone else's, but she realized that the strange business of the open verdict was keeping Rosabelle in London and it was to her advantage to keep that fear alive.

From then on Rosabelle became even more reclusive and made no friends outside the workplace. Her natural reserve and ever-present feeling of inadequacy made her deliberately withdraw to the background when clients came to Half Moon Street and so, more and more, she took on the position of an onlooker.

Most of the clients were in awe of Rachelle, though not deceived by her affectations. In their transactions, however, she always won. Time and again the same scene was enacted. A customer would try to protest, 'Madame Rachelle, you're asking too much for this gown. Your prices are scandalously high. Can't you offer something cheaper for a good client?' This perpetual refrain could be spoken in the voice of confident privilege, but Rachelle only looked down her nose at them.

'Cheaper, madame? You're looking for cheapness?' The look in her eye spoke volumes and usually the client quailed, but not always. It was only an exceptionally strong-minded woman who could stand up against this scorn. Most of them caved in.

'I've spent two hundred pounds here in the past year. My husband is making a fuss. He says that I must patronize another *modiste* . . . in Paris perhaps,' said a bold American.

Rachelle's lip curled. 'But your husband is a peer. Have you asked how much he spends at the gaming tables?' And she calmly folded up the coveted gown, nodding to a sales-girl to take it away, before saying, 'If it is cheapness you are after, my lady, I'll be happy to provide you with the address

of another dressmaker . . . but when you go out in society, I'd
be obliged if you point out that your clothes no longer come
from us. We have a *reputation* to maintain, you see.'

After watching this scene, Rosabelle said to Rachelle,
'Weren't you a little hard on her? One hundred guineas for
that dress is very steep.'

Rachelle laughed. 'She can afford it. Her father builds
bridges or something in America and bought her a duke for
a husband. Besides, she shouldn't have argued with me the
way she did, threatening to go to Paris for her clothes!' But
when she saw that Rosabelle was concerned, she put a hand
on her arm and said consolingly, 'Don't worry. When we
ask these women to pay ridiculous prices, they think we're
special. They like giving their money to the most expensive
dressmaker in town.'

Some customers were intrigued by the blonde young
woman who they knew created the designs they so coveted.
One or two made friendly overtures, or asked where she
came from, because they noticed her unusual accent though
she spoke as little as possible.

She was never specific. 'I'm from Scotland,' she'd say
with a smile, but never provided more details.

One young matron was sufficiently impressed by
Rosabelle's silent dignity to invite her to tea in Belgrave
Square, and was taken aback when the invitation was
hurriedly refused.

'I'm sorry. I can't,' said Rosabelle.

'What about another day then? I'd be so pleased if you
would come and meet my mother and a few of my friends.
I've been telling them how clever you are . . .'

Rosabelle was in an obvious state of confusion. 'I can't.
I'm sorry. I'm too busy.'

The thought of going out to tea in Belgrave Square terrified her because she was afraid she wouldn't manage her
teaspoon or cake fork properly or know the right way to fold
her napkin. The social gap between Eyemouth and Belgrave
Square was too wide.

She found the outside world increasingly intimidating and had to force herself to venture even as far as Piccadilly. In a strange way the surging noise of traffic all around made her think of the sea and she was repelled by the memory. Sometimes she only managed to go a short distance before faintness overwhelmed her and she hurried back home, sweating and shaking.

Work became her refuge, and loneliness a self-imposed part of her life. She often thought longingly of Jessie, remembering how they used to laugh and gossip together. It seemed a long time since she had really laughed.

If Jessie materialized at that moment, what would they do? Where would they go? With Jessie beside her, would she have the courage to venture out into London's crowded streets? What was Effie doing? she wondered. Cooking, probably. Was Jessie making jokes? And Aaron, her son, what about him?

Guilt always swept over her when she thought about the little boy. Good mothers did not desert their children.

I'm not very maternal; some women aren't, she thought as she tried to find an excuse for herself. *I didn't really desert him! I left him with someone who loves him better than I do, and I send money – more money in a month than the disaster fund provides for him in a year.*

When Rachelle noticed that her partner was under stress, she took care to coddle her, putting potted plants and vases of flowers in the studio and ordering blazing fires to be lit in the grate at any sign of bad weather. At all costs, Rosabelle must be kept comfortable, for both their futures were invested in her – and Rachelle was fond of her, as fond as she was of any woman.

'I hate to see you wasting your life,' she said one day when Rosabelle refused to accompany her for a drive in the park.

'I don't want to go out,' was always the reply.

'Why not? Have you another engagement?'

'No. I . . . I don't like going out.'

'You might as well be in a nunnery. You should find your-self another husband, and you won't find one if you never go out,' scolded Rachelle.

'Please don't pester me. I don't want another husband. Dan was my husband and he died . . .' Besides, in Rosabelle's mind the streets of London seemed full of predatory men like Anderson. It was safest to stay at home.

Creating lovely clothes was her solace. The designs were cut out and stitched up by outworkers scattered all over London, and only the most expensive materials went to the three women in Whitechapel. Eth, the eldest, regularly came to Half Moon Street to collect or deliver the latest assignment and, over time, struck up a cheerful relationship with Rosabelle.

One afternoon, awaiting the arrival of a dreamlike gown embroidered with scrolls of seed pearls, Rosabelle rushed to the front door when she heard the rumble of carriage wheels outside. A rough-looking young man in a floppy cloth cap and red neckerchief was climbing down from a cab with an enormous cardboard box. Eth followed him and when she saw Rosabelle her face split wide in a grin.

''Ello, ducks. You've scored a bullseye this time. This one's lovely,' she cried cheerfully.

The young man laid the dress box on the floor and Eth reverently pulled out yards and yards of glittering, chinking material. Rosabelle loved the moment when her ideas were translated into reality and she stood with hands clasped and eyes dancing as Eth held the dress against her own body and said, 'Good, ain't it?'

'Magnificent,' Rosabelle said in delight, tenderly touching the fabric and admiring the way the vision in her head had been brought to life. She felt as proud as if she'd painted the ceiling of the Sistine Chapel.

'Glad you're pleased. Where's Sadie? I hope she feels the same. She's always trying to cut down our money,' was Eth's reply.

'Do you mean Rachelle? Why do you call her Sadie?' Rosabelle asked.

Eth laughed. 'Because that's her name. All that Rachelle de Roquefort stuff is just balderdash.' Eth was in a chatty mood.

'What *is* her real name?' Rosabelle asked.

'You mean she hasn't told you? It's the same as mine.'

'And what's that?'

'Richardson. She's Sadie Richardson and I was Ethel Richardson before I married Charlie Watts, God rest 'im.'

'Are you related?'

Eth threw back her head and laughed. 'God bless you, she's my sister. Don't we look like each other? This lad here is her son Stanley.' She pointed at the thug by her side. He shuffled his feet and grinned.

Her son! So Rachelle had a son. Rosabelle felt herself go cold. The lad looked about eighteen, dark-haired and thickset, unshaven and uncouth. If anyone had considered grabbing the pearl-embroidered gown off Eth as she rode through the East End, they'd think twice when they saw Rachelle's son on the cab's box.

'Does he live with you?' Rosabelle asked.

'Yeah. I've had 'im since he was born. I love 'im though he can be trouble at times.' Eth spoke about Stanley as if he was deaf.

'Does he know you're not his mother? Does he know it's Rachelle?' Rosabelle's tone was urgent.

Eth looked at her curiously, wondering why she was so upset. 'Yeah. Stan's always known. Ain't that right, Stan?' He was being included in the conversation now.

'Do you care? Does it matter to you?' When Rosabelle spoke to Stan there was a strange entreaty in her voice.

'Why should I? I'm better off with Eth,' he mumbled.

'Sadie was only a kid when she 'ad 'im. She couldn't drag 'im round with 'er. 'E'd have cramped her style,' Eth said as if that was explanation enough.

Rosabelle's eyes were full of tears and, seeing how upset

she was, Eth lifted up the gown and said, 'For God's sake don't start blubbing over this dress. There's nothing to cry about.'

Feeling foolish, Rosabelle pulled herself together, managed a smile and said, 'Of course not – it's just that I miss my family . . .'

'You should get out more. Sadie says you don't put a foot over the door from one week's end to the next. You'll go funny if you don't look out,' said Eth sharply as she hung the dress up on a rail where it swung like a banner.

When the callers left, Rosabelle stood at the door to watch them getting back into the cab and saw Eth look up into the young man's face and laugh. He laughed too and put an arm affectionately over her shoulders.

Rosabelle then sat down at her drawing board and wept bitterly. She was still weeping when Rachelle came home.

'What's wrong? Has that fool Eth messed up the dress?' was her first question when she saw Rosabelle's swollen eyes.

'No. It's lovely. She brought it a few hours ago and it's on the display rail now.'

Rachelle ran downstairs to see it and Rosabelle heard her exclamations of delight. When she came back she declared, 'It's your best yet. I'm going to ask two hundred for it. Aren't you pleased? What's wrong? You look as if you've been at a funeral.'

Rosabelle gave a little gulp and a sob. 'Eth told me your real name and she introduced me to your son.'

'To Stan?'

'Yes.'

'What of it? Was he rude to you?'

'No, of course he wasn't. He seems a nice boy.'

'Then what's wrong? Is it because you didn't know my name? But if you were called Sadie, wouldn't you want to change it?'

Rosabelle shook her head. 'I'm sad because Stanley made me think of my own son.'

37

Rachelle walked across the room to light one of her cigarettes from a taper she stuck into the fire. 'I don't think there can be much similarity between them.'

'I mean, like me, you gave your baby away. You never told me that. I feel so guilty about Aaron . . .'

'I don't. Stan was better off being brought up by someone else. The three women you met in Whitechapel are my sisters and they love him, Eth most of all. He thinks of her as his mother. It would have been cruel to take him away from her, even after I began to make money.'

'Have you ever felt sorry?' It obviously mattered to Rosabelle.

'To be perfectly honest, no. Some women are not maternal and I'm one of them. I was only sixteen when I had him and wasn't even sure who his father was, though now I see Stan grown up, I have a good idea. I gave my baby to Eth because she'd lost a little girl a few months before, and was grieving.'

'*Gave* him – it wasn't a loan or anything like that?'

'You don't *loan* a baby. You make up your mind and give him away. I wanted out of Whitechapel. I hated it there. My sisters tried to make me a dressmaker like them, but I wasn't up to their standard, though I can tell good work and good designs when I see them,' said Rachelle.

'How did you manage to leave?'

Rosabelle drew on her cigarette and her expression seemed distant as she remembered. 'Oh, I was wild when I was young. I used to hang round the theatres, mending costumes and things like that. One day I was offered a part in the chorus, dancing and kicking up my legs. I loved dressing up and painting my face. I did that till I gave birth to Stan, but I missed the theatre, so I gave him to Eth, changed my name and went back on the road with the company. Nobody but my sisters have ever called me Sadie since.'

She paused and looked sharply at Rosabelle. 'I understand what you're going through about your little boy. When I had mine, I reckoned that if I wanted a decent life, I had to get away. I think it was easier to give him up because I never breastfed him. I hadn't any milk.'

'I didn't feed Aaron either,' whispered Rosabelle. Perhaps Rachelle was right; perhaps that was why she too had been able to give her son up.

She knew she must go back one day to put her mind at ease. But once she got home, would she want to stay there after all that had happened?

Five

'*Thank you for the money. It came by one of those new postal orders. You are always too generous. Aaron and I don't need so much. I am glad you are well and busy. Old Willie Wake is still alive and singing his daft songs . . .*'

Effie was bent over her table, carefully penning a letter, when Jessie came bouncing in and looked over her shoulder. 'Is that to Rosabelle?' she asked.

'Yes,' was the short reply.

'Send her my love. Say that I miss her.'

Effie looked over her shoulder with a frown and asked, 'And will I tell her that you're expecting another baby?'

Jessie was only silent for a moment before she grinned and asked, 'How did you know that?'

'I smell it. I've always been able to tell if a woman's pregnant, sometimes before she knows it herself.' Effie's voice was bleak but Jessie was not abashed.

'You're right this time too,' was her blithe reply.

'So can I tell Rosabelle the name of the father and if you're getting married soon?'

'You can make it up if you like,' Jessie teased.

'Who *is* the father?' Effie asked, laying down her pen.

Jessie picked up Henrietta from her cradle, cuddled her tight and laughed. 'That's my secret and I'm not telling.'

Like the last time, her pregnancy became evident at an early stage and everyone was asking the same question: 'Who fathered Jessie's bairn?'

Theories abounded. The owner of the livery stable was

40

suggested. After all, hadn't she fixed up her brother Pat with a job there, and every time she saw him he saluted her extravagantly, frequently giving her a pillion ride home on his horse.

However, the gossips' favourite candidate was Reverend Alan Cochrane. He was surprised when the congregation at his Sunday morning services suddenly increased, and could not understand why the people packed into the pews had become so much more attentive. They sat forward and followed every word he uttered with fixed attention. Was Eyemouth undergoing some sort of religious revival? he wondered.

Effie was quick to discus the matter with her friend Euphen.

'Alex's awful upset about Mr Cochrane,' Euphen said.

'Why?' Effie had not heard the rumours about the minister and Jessie.

'Alex always thought Mr Cochrane was a good man, the best of the ministers in this town, but now he's gone and done this . . .'

'Heavens above, what's he done?'

'Folk are saying he's the father of Jessie's bairn. He's forever in Stanhope's mooning around the cheese counter, and when she smiles at him he goes the colour of beet-root.'

Effie shook her head. 'I don't believe it. Jessie wouldn't go for him . . . He's sort of *soft*, isn't he?'

'You can never tell. Look at the Prince of Wales. He's soft-looking and you know what they say about him. Has Jessie ever given you a hint about the father?'

Effie shook her head. 'Not a word, but whoever it is, she was willing, I can tell you that.'

'Maybe it was somebody off a foreign fishing boat. There was one in from Holland a couple of months ago . . . Like Rosabelle's mother, you know. Once they're away, they don't care about what they've left behind.'

'I heard something about the livery stable man, and the

41

maid at the Royal Hotel thought it might be that Everard Stanhope, the lawyer from Edinburgh. He always speaks a lot to Jessie when he comes home,' said Effie.

'He's more likely than Mr Cochrane,' agreed Euphen, and went away contented because she thought Effie had dropped her a deliberate hint.

Next time Jessie came for Henrietta, Effie was on the offensive. 'Everybody's wondering about your bairn's father, Jessie. They've been suggesting all sorts of names, from Mr Stanhope's lawyer son to Mr Cochrane the minister.'

Jessie laughed. 'Mr Cochrane! Poor soul. He goes bright red every time he asks me for a bit of cheese. I doubt if he's ever been to bed with a woman. It's none of their business. Don't worry. We'll be all right – me and Henrietta and the new baby – and you too; I'll see to that.'

Jessie liked being pregnant. She enjoyed the feeling of another person growing inside her; and felt a thrill of pleasure as the child heaved round and its leg or arm made a bulge like a wave rising in her belly. She felt a kinship with the child long before it was born, and talked to her bulge when she was alone as if it was already in her arms.

Soon it was difficult to fit into her clothes and her dresses were impossible to fasten completely. At work she swathed a big apron around her waist to make the bulge look smaller.

It was a problem for Jessie when her sister Mary announced that she'd set the day for her marriage. 'I've waited long enough,' she told Jessie, who nodded in agreement.

'God knows how you've held out so long, Mary.'

'Because I wanted it to be right,' said Mary, and Jessie sighed.

'What's right, what's wrong? I've always had trouble with that, but I'm glad for you. Where's it to be?'

'Lamberton Toll, next Wednesday. He'll come up with his party and we'll meet him there. I want to keep it small. Fanny can't come because her next bairn's due next week. It'll just be you and me and the wee ones from our side.'

Jessie clapped her hands. 'Grand! I just hope I can still fit into the dress I wore at Fanny's wedding. I want to look my best.'

The dress turned out to be a tight fit and a lot of pinning and tacking was required to get Jessie into it, but the big hat was as splendid as ever when she took it out of its box. The dark purple feathers on the bird's breast still glistened like silk, and when she perched it on her head, she preened as she remembered Rosabelle and the French woman saying it was good enough for the Palace.

Like when Fanny got married, the bride's family went to Lamberton Toll on the early morning of the wedding, riding on the carrier's cart.

The journey was short and the marriage ceremony brief. All that was required was for the couple to affirm in front of the tollkeeper that neither of them was already married, and that they intended to take each other as man and wife.

Mary's new husband was a fine-looking young fellow, and it was all Jessie could do to stop herself from making eyes at him as the couple signed the tollkeeper's register.

Outside in the sunshine the guests congratulated the couple, and the groom suggested that they all cram into his big carriage to go to Berwick station from where he and Mary would catch the train to his hometown. He said he would buy tickets for Mary's relatives to catch the next train to Burnmouth.

'It'll be quicker and more comfortable than going home with the carrier,' he said. Everyone was happy to accept a free train ride from the generous groom. Only Jessie hung back.

'There won't be enough room in your cab for all of us. I take up too much space now so I'll just wait here for the carrier coming back,' she said.

Mary looked at her with concern, remembering how

quickly Jessie gave birth to her last baby. 'But the carrier's not coming back for an hour. Will you be all right?' she asked.

'Perhaps somebody else'll come along. They often do.'

'For you, they do,' agreed Mary.

The wedding party was not long gone when a gig drew up outside the tollhouse and a man got out. Jessie rose from her seat by the wall and walked across to meet him, taking his arm affectionately and smiling into his face. It was obvious she'd been waiting for him to turn up.

Although she kept threatening to leave for the South of France, Hester did not seem capable of tearing herself away from Eyemouth. First, post-delivery malaise held her up, and then baby Louisa developed croup just as they were about to travel.

In fact, the real reason for her staying at home was because she was still trying to find out what had happened to her husband on the night he died. She brooded on the matter, but dared not open the subject with her father, to whom she barely spoke.

They had never been close, and Mr Stanhope did not seem to mind his daughter's withdrawal from him. In fact, she minded it more than he did as she often discovered a choice bit of gossip that she longed to share with him, but could not because she was the one who was keeping her distance.

Pushing her baby in a big-wheeled perambulator, she went round gossiping with friends who nodded sympathetically as she talked obsessively about Anderson's murder, but in fact they thought she was becoming deranged about him, and tried to divert her with other bits of news. It was her friend, the wife of the Episcopal Church minister, who told her the gossip about Mr Cochrane and Jessie.

She was galvanized with curiosity at the thought that an illicit affair was being conducted over her father's cheese counter. Her face was transformed. 'Is it true?' she asked.

Her friend nodded with pursed lips. 'A scandal indeed!' she affirmed.

Hester hurried off to the store and as soon as she set foot across the threshold, she spotted Jessie's bulging belly sticking out under the white apron.

The two women looked at each other and Hester's face was thunderous as she asked, 'Mrs Maltman or Miss whatever-you're-called, shouldn't you be resting at home in your condition?'

'I'm very well, thank you,' said Jessie innocently.

Hester stalked along the length of the counter and headed for her father's office at the far end of the building. He was sitting in his swivel chair in front of a large roll-top desk with a glass of what looked like sherry on a small table beside him.

His daughter looked at it askance. 'Drinking, Father, at this time in the morning?' she asked.

'I take a small amontillado now and again. It's good for my heart. Jessie brings it to me when she thinks I'm looking tired.'

Hester snorted. 'Jessie! She's what I want to talk to you about. It is most unseemly for an unmarried woman of doubtful reputation to be serving our customers in such a shocking state. Especially considering who people are saying fathered her child.'

He looked surprised. 'Unseemly? Man? What man?'

She sneered. 'Don't act silly, Father. There has to be some man involved. It's that trollop Jessie, of course. Respectable women do not allow themselves to be seen in public when they are as *big* as that girl. My friends will take their custom elsewhere if they come in here and see her.'

'But you said she isn't respectable. Anyway, your friends, and women with equally acute sensibilities, don't usually come into the shop themselves; they send servants with their orders. The girl needs the money,' said her father. It was obvious that he did not give a fig about Jessie's condition.

'Probably, but it's scandalous for anyone to display herself in such a state of *fecundity*! Like an animal. She looks like a pumpkin. And she's not even married. She wasn't married to that fisherman who drowned, though she claims relief money for him and for her other child. Steven told me that!'

'She might have got married since,' said her father mildly, lifting his sherry glass and taking a sip.

'If she has, it isn't to the man people are saying is the father of this child she's carrying.' Hester was stuttering and almost incoherent with fury.

'How do you know that? Has she told you?' asked Stanhope

'Of course not. It's Mr Cochrane, a minister of the Church! Don't you think that's a scandal? It'll ruin him.'

Her father actually laughed and raised himself a little from his chair so he could look through the clear glass on the top of his office door. Jessie was leaning on the counter, smiling at the very man they were talking about.

'Actually I suspect it'll do his reputation a lot of good,' he said.

'Don't be stupid,' snapped his daughter. 'I'm going out there to dismiss her and tell her to go home.'

A thunderous look came into her father's eye and there was steel in his voice when he said, 'I don't think you should do that, Hester.'

She glared back at him. 'I've never liked that girl. She's got you twisted round her little finger. I'd have sent her packing long ago but you wanted to keep her on. She can get the father of her baby – whoever he is – to keep her now.'

'Don't be so hard. Even if you don't like the girl, that's no reason to persecute her. When she has to go, I'll be the one to tell her because, as long as I'm alive, I'm the head of this family and of all my shops. When I'm gone you can do as you like, but not till then,' he said firmly.

It was clear that Hester could do nothing, and so she

46

stamped out of his office in a rage. As she passed the couple at the cheese counter, she stared rudely at Cochrane and asked loudly, 'Are you not ashamed? A man of God, behaving like an *animal*!'

He looked at her in astonishment as the words 'Good morning, Miss Stanhope' died on his lips. Turning, he watched her disappearing through the main door and, when he turned back, he realized that everybody in the shop was looking at him. Jessie was laughing, her eyes dancing with glee.

'What did she mean?' he asked her.

She beckoned with one hooked finger to bring his head close to hers, then she leaned across the cheese and whispered in his ear. 'She's saying you're the father of the bairn I'm having.'

He looked into the dancing dark eyes and whispered back, 'Is that what she thinks?' Jessie nodded and ogled him in a way that made his heart jump.

When he straightened up, he seemed to have become taller and more self-assured. As he left the shop, he smiled at the other curious shoppers, and, carrying his cheese, felt as potent and powerful as a king.

Furious and seething, Hester was waiting for her father when he arrived home that evening. 'I will not put up with being treated in such a shaming way by you,' she told him.

He did not apologize. 'Why don't you take that holiday in France, my dear? I'll pay,' he said instead.

She spent the next week packing her boxes and travelling trunks, and took off for an indefinite stay with her baby and its nursemaid at Menton.

Her father was relieved to see her go.

Just before dawn on a crisp autumn morning, Jessie went into labour, and young Betsy ran to fetch Effie, who arrived leading a sleepy Aaron by the hand.

'It's started,' Jessie calmly told her when she appeared in the bedroom doorway.

'All right. I'll put Aaron to bed with your Betsy, and then I'll fetch Euphen.'

This time there was no shouting, and little pain. After less than two hours the baby was delivered. It was another girl. Both of the women who'd helped with the birth examined its little face with keen interest, then looked at each other and silently shook their heads in disappointment. They could discern no likeness to anyone they knew except the mother.

Jessie was radiant when the baby was put in her arms.

'What are you going to call her?' Effie asked.

Jessie looked down into the little face. The child had black curls like hers and the same round, pink cheeks.

'I'm going to call her Poppy,' she said. 'Poppy Johnston,' she added mischievously, looking at the curious women round her bed.

One goes out when another comes in.

People trotted out the old saying as they talked about Jessie's new baby and speculated about its parentage.

And, as if on cue, when Poppy Johnston made her entry into the world, Willie Wake was on his way out.

Although the people of the town fed and clothed the old man no one was exactly sure of his age. Scarecrow-thin and wild-eyed, he roamed the pier head, accosting people and singing crazy songs.

It was a relief to Jessie when his memory began to fade. He told her he couldn't recall what happened yesterday; he didn't remember the names of people he'd known since they were children, but, perversely, the last thing he forgot was his favourite song about the devil coming out on a cold black night.

If Jessie heard him singing it, she always stopped and scolded him. 'I don't like that song. Sing something else, Willie.'

Poppy was forty-eight hours old on the day he died. Coastguard Duncan found him lying semi-conscious in the door of the net shed and when Willie saw him bending down to help him up, he grabbed Duncan's hand and cried, 'Duncan, Duncan, get me a meenister. I want to say my prayers.'

Reverend Alan Cochrane was fetched and knelt by the old man lying on a pile of rags.

'Say a prayer for me,' said Willie.

Cochrane cradled the old man's head and began, 'Yea though I walk through the valley of death . . .'

Willie croaked anxiously, 'Not that. Say something to stop me goin' to Hell.'

'You're not going to Hell, Willie. You've never done anything bad,' said Cochrane gently.

'Aye, I have. I pushed the relief man aff the pier. He didnae fall, I pushed him.'

The two men who were with him stared at each other and, when Willie died a short time later, Duncan said to Cochrane, 'I don't think I heard anything about the relief man.'

As Cochrane gently closed Willie's eyes, he nodded and said, 'Neither did I.'

When she wrote her weekly letter to Rosabelle, Effie had important news to tell . . .

> Old Willie Wake is dead at last. His mind went years ago, but every now and again he'd come out with a flash of sense that surprised people. I'll never forget how he warned the boats not to go out on Black Friday. If only they'd listened to him. He died in the net shed where he's lived since that Collin woman, his daughter-in-law, put him out of the house. Mr Cochrane was with him at the end and held his burial service in the big church yesterday. A lot of people turned out for it.

When the letter was read out to her, Rosabelle jumped up in her chair and cried out, 'Is Willie Wake really dead?'

Rachelle's eyebrows went up in surprise. 'Didn't you like him?'

'Oh, it's not that. He was a decent old man. A poor old thing, in fact . . .'

She was not going to tell Rachelle that he'd taken her secret with him to the grave, and so had set her free.

There was nothing to stop Rosabelle going home now if she wanted. Seven years had passed and she could go back to see the son she only remembered as a baby. What was he like? Tall or short? Clever or stupid? Would he know who she was when they met?

Six

Stan often delivered dresses to Half Moon Street from the women in Whitechapel, and every time she saw him Rosabelle watched the way he greeted his real mother.

They seemed little more than acquaintances. He always called her 'Sadie' and made jokes that made her laugh. Sometimes she even tipped him, as she would tip an ordinary delivery boy.

'How often did you see Stan when he was growing up?' she asked Rachelle.

'How often? Not a lot. Every couple of years or so.'

'Did that make you feel sad or guilty?'

'No, why should it? I knew he was better off with Eth. What's bothering you?'

'It's a long time since I saw my son . . . seven years. Time has passed so fast.'

Rachelle was unable to hide her expression of alarm and that made Rosabelle realize how crucial she was to the success of their partnership. Until now she'd felt that Rachelle was the important one. The knowledge surprised her.

'So?' said Rachelle challengingly.

'I think I ought to go home.'

A dark look passed over Rachelle's face. 'For good?' she asked cautiously.

'No, I don't think so. But I want to see Aaron. I've no idea what he looks like now. He was just a baby; he couldn't even speak properly when I left him.'

'You'd have heard if there was anything wrong with him,

and he must have changed – children do in seven years,' Rachelle said in an attempt at lightheartedness.

'I know. I want to see what he's changed into.'

Rachelle grimaced. 'Sometimes it's best to keep separate from your children. I'd no idea you were so worried about your boy. Do you want me to go back to Scotland with you?'

Is she afraid that I might never come back? Rosabelle wondered. 'It's best if I go on my own,' she said aloud. 'Will you write to Effie for me, please, and tell her that I'm coming home?'

Rosabelle's train was late when it pulled into Burnmouth station. Effie, waiting on the platform, was little changed, slightly greyer perhaps but as four-square and determined as ever. Her eyes looked anxious as she scanned the passengers descending from the train and at first she did not recognize the slim woman in her smart travelling costume of a tight-fitting jacket with a peplum over the hips, and a long flowing skirt of soft grey flannel. It was only the curling yellow hair beneath the brim of the woman's hat that gave her a clue. She held out her arms and cried, 'Oh my dear lass!'

Sobbing too, Rosabelle stepped into the embrace and they hugged each other tight. It was as if they had only been apart for days instead of years.

Watching their reunion was a wary-looking, dark-eyed boy. He'd been told a lot about this stranger who was his mother and had been warned to be on his best behaviour. With one hand he touched Effie's skirt and leaned towards her for protection, though he wanted to seem big and manly.

Rosabelle dropped to her knees in front of him, careless that dust from the platform stained the front of her immaculate skirt. Tears ran down her cheeks but he stared at her without any expression.

'Is this Aaron?' she asked, though she would have known him even if she met him on a London street. He was so like Dan.

'I'm Aaron,' he said stiffly.

'I'm your mother,' she replied, holding out her arms.

He turned his head away and looked at Effie. 'No, my mother's here,' he said, leaning even closer into her.

'No, no,' said Effie. 'You know I'm your grandmother.' When she and the boy looked at each other, his hostile attitude disappeared and love filled both their faces.

It shouldn't have been like this. If it wasn't for that awful storm my son would look at me in the same way as he's looking at Effie, thought Rosabelle. She wanted to hug her son but was afraid that if she touched him, he would recoil from her. She was also afraid that touching him would be like touching Dan, for the child was his living image, too like his father for her peace of mind.

One goes out when one comes in, she thought bitterly, and remembered her conviction that Dan's death was a sort of pagan sacrifice so that this child could live.

As she stood up, she saw him staring at her as if he sensed her reservations.

'I'm your mother. I've come from London on a visit, and I have presents for you in my bag,' she said in what she hoped was a lighthearted voice.

The boy said nothing.

The day was brilliant, warm and sunny with glittering highlights dancing on an aquamarine sea, so the walk from the station to Eyemouth was pleasant, but when they came in sight of the bay, Rosabelle dropped her head in an effort not to stare across the water to the Hurkar Rocks which still jutted up out of the water, as sinister and hateful as ever.

Avoidance was impossible. She had to look. They drew her eyes. Every crack and crevice of them seemed to stand out in high relief. Again she saw Dan clinging to the biggest rock, waving in his desperate fight for life.

The pain that seized her heart was agonizing. The intervening years disappeared and she was back there, staring at his terrible death scene.

'Oh no!' she groaned, cutting off the sight of the rocks by covering her eyes with gloved hands.

Effie patted her shoulder as if she understood, but the boy stared from one to the other, perplexed. What's the matter with her? he wondered.

Later, in Effie's kitchen, she collected herself sufficiently to try to talk to her son again. 'Do you go to school, Aaron?' she asked.

'Yes, m'm,' he said. With guile he was attempting to avoid actually calling her 'mother' or 'mum'. He and Henrietta called Effie 'mam', and it seemed to him to be a sort of betrayal to call this stranger by any name that sounded like that.

'What are you good at?' she asked next.

He shuffled his feet, and Effie chipped in with the information that he was very good at art. Rosabelle brightened and smiled at him. 'Do you draw pictures?'

He shook his head and again it was Effie who spoke. 'He carves things out of bits of wood picked up on the shore. I'll show you some later. He's very artistic, like you,' she said proudly.

'Do you want to be a sculptor?' she asked him but he shook his head. 'No, I'm going to the fishing when I'm old enough.'

'He'll have his own boat once he's learned the ropes. He has almost enough money to buy a share in one already, thanks to you. I've saved nearly every penny you've sent us,' said Effie proudly.

Rosabelle flinched and thought it ironic that her money would help her son do the one thing she never wanted him to do.

On Effie's mantelpiece stood a photograph of four proud-looking men in sea boots standing beside their boat. Jimmy Dip's lucky stone swung on the nail at the back of the door, still knocking against the wood every time the door was opened. Was it waiting for Aaron to touch it before he sailed off to his death? Rosabelle wondered, with terrible fear.

Seeing her distress, Effie nudged the boy and told him to let his mother see some of his carvings. He went out for a moment and came back carrying an armful of strangely shaped twigs. They were pieces of driftwood, rubbed down to a fine sheen – some silver coloured, others yellow like gold.

She picked one up and saw it was a flower with a drooping head on a long stalk; another was a yapping dog.

'These are lovely! Did you make them?' she cried, and when he nodded, she bent down to hug him, only to feel him stiffen under her arms.

As she released him, she looked up and saw someone else standing in the open doorway. 'Jessie!' she cried and ran towards her friend.

Jessie was plumper, but still pretty as a peach – though soon she would be overripe, thought Rosabelle. With her was a brown-haired girl that had to be Henrietta, and in her arms a sleeping infant.

Rosabelle peeled the shawl back from the baby's face. 'Is this your mystery child?' she asked.

Jessie giggled. 'Effie's been writing you letters! There's no mystery, she came the usual way.'

Rosabelle laughed too. If Jessie wanted to tell her more, she would. Otherwise she would hold her tongue and ask no questions. It was Jessie's business, and she could see that the woman Jessie had become could cope with that very well.

They all sat at the kitchen table drinking tea, talking as if she had never been away, with Effie and Jessie taking turns to fill Rosabelle in on the town gossip.

Henrietta was helping Aaron with his carvings, and though she was only six weeks older than him, she treated him in a motherly way and he carved a piece of wood into a tiny sheep for her. While he was working on it, Rosabelle leaned over to watch. It was a jaunty-looking animal with its tail sticking up like a flag, and as she watched her son's capable little hands holding the whittling knife she felt a rush of fellow feeling for him. Like her, he knew the joy of creation, the joy of seeing something growing under your hands.

She was jerked back to the others by Jessie asking a question. 'How's your Clara?'

'It's not been easy to keep in touch with her, but a few years ago she sent me a letter to say Tom's doing well. He's a police lieutenant in Boston and they have two children – a boy and a girl. She wants me to go out and visit her,' she told them.

'Will you go?' asked Jessie, who would set sail for Boston without a moment's hesitation provided she was sure of coming back again, but Rosabelle shook her head.

'I don't think so. I can't imagine what she's like now, because I can't read or write and it's difficult to get any *feeling* from letters when they're read to you or written for you by someone else.'

There was another reason she'd decided against going to America. She hated the sea so much that the thought of setting foot in a boat and crossing the ocean appalled her.

'I know what you mean,' said Jessie. 'I cannae read or write either, but I can count up. There's somebody else I was wondering about – that French woman, the one with the fancy name – Rachelle? How's she? Is she playing fair with you?'

It struck Rosabelle that neither Jessie nor Effie had any idea of what her life in London was like, or the sort of money that was paid for the things she designed. It was as if she was acting in a play – but what was real: London or here?

'Rachelle's an excellent businesswoman. I owe her a lot,' she said carefully.

Before Jessie went home she asked Rosabelle to call in and see her at Stanhope's grocery the next day. 'I want the rest of the folk in the shop to see what a grand lady you've become,' she said.

After she left, Effie asked, 'Who do you think the baby looks like? She'll not tell me who the father is, and some folk say it's that long thin minister, Mr Cochrane. They walk

56

round the town together because he's writing a book, and she tells him all the old stories she heard from her father and grandmother. I think she invents half of it, but he laps them up.'

'I thought the baby looks like her. It's going to be another Jessie,' said Rosabelle.

'And Aaron's another Dan,' said Effie, fondly looking at the little boy, but when she saw the look on Rosabelle's face, she wished she'd kept her mouth shut.

During the night Rosabelle woke in the deep feather bed and lay listening to the sea. Loud and insistent, it surged and murmured, reminding her of its power. She hated it.

After breakfast next day, Effie suggested that Aaron take his mother round the town. 'Look in on Mrs Lyall, and most of all, please call in on Euphen. She's not been well but she wants to see you,' she said.

They set off in bright sunshine and her son was polite, but ill at ease, so conversation between them was heart-breakingly difficult. He was more at ease with other people than he was with his mother.

Mrs Lyall was as eagle-eyed and sharp as ever, enviously eyeing Rosabelle's smart clothes. She patted Aaron's head and said, 'You must be proud at the way he's turning out, but he doesn't resemble you much, does he?'

Rosabelle only nodded.

At Stanhope's grocery Jessie, resplendent in a vast white apron that seemed as stiff as a carapace of armour, screamed with delight when they stepped inside and introduced Rosabelle to all the other shop workers. Mr Stanhope stood up and peered over his door to catch a sight of her, but did not come out.

As they were leaving, Jessie, with a grandiose gesture, bestowed a paper bag of candied orange peel on Aaron, and said to Rosabelle, 'That's his favourite. Remember the time I brought some home and you liked it too?' Rosabelle smiled and nodded but realized sadly that she, Aaron's mother, had no idea about his likes or dislikes.

Their last call was on Euphen. Her house, unlike her husband's boat, had always been immaculately clean, so Rosabelle was surprised to find dishes littering the table, and the hearth that used to glitter like quicksilver was dull and badly in need of black leading. Unlike Effie, Euphen had aged. Her face was deeply lined and her back bent as if she was protecting some inner part of herself from pain.

Her smile was as sweet and reassuring as ever, however. 'How bonny you are. You were always a pretty lassie but now you're a beauty. Wouldn't your mother be proud of you!' she said.

It was a long time since Rosabelle had thought about her mother and her eyes now filled with tears.

'Don't cry,' said kind Euphen. 'Sit down and tell me about your life in London.'

To her own surprise, Rosabelle poured out the story of Rachelle – real name Sadie – and her family history. She even told her how Rachelle had given away her son and never regretted having done so. Euphen never interrupted or offered advice, so it was like confessing to a priest, and Rosabelle heard herself saying things that she was not aware of even thinking.

'I don't know what's wrong with me. I don't seem to feel happy or at ease anywhere. The only time I'm not sad is when I'm working . . .'

Euphen patted her hand and said, 'You're still grieving. It takes some people a long time to get over a loss like yours . . . But it will get better. It will.'

After Aaron went to bed that night, Effie built up the fire in the big cast-iron range and gestured to Rosabelle to sit in Jimmy Dip's old seat that was only offered to special visitors.

'Have you come home for good?' was her first question, for it had been uppermost in her mind ever since she saw Rosabelle on the station platform.

'No, I can't stay because I don't want to let Rachelle down. We've built up a good business. If it goes on for a few more years we'll be rich,' was Rosabelle's reply, but she did not add that she felt uncomfortable in Eyemouth. There was still too much sadness all around for her.

'Then when you're rich, will you come back and start a sewing business like Mrs Lyall's?' Effie could not imagine the extent or sophistication of Rosabelle's work.

'I might not have to work at all,' was her reply.

'Fancy that! You've done well for yourself,' said Effie in admiration.

'Not yet though,' said Rosabelle with a laugh. But soon she became serious again. 'You've brought up Aaron well, Effie. No one could have done as good a job as you.'

'He's my precious laddie. I love him with all my heart,' said Effie, looking hard into Rosabelle's face, as if pleading with her not to take him away.

'I can see he's very happy with you and I want him to have the best of everything. Am I sending you enough money?' Rosabelle asked.

'Far more than we need. He wants for nothing. Alex Burgon says that when he's old enough, he'll get him a share in a really good boat. As I told you, I've saved enough for that already, thanks to you.'

Rosabelle swallowed, turned her face away and looked into the heart of the fire before she said, 'I don't want him to go to sea.'

Effie was shocked. 'Not go to sea! But all the men of both our families have gone to sea. It's in his blood. He wants to go. He watches the boats; he knows all the fish and forecasts the weather. He must go to sea. That's why I fought for us to keep our bairns in Eyemouth, and not send them off to Quarrier's home. They'll build the town back to what it was before the storm.'

She was referring to the attempt of the disaster fund trustees to send the fatherless children of Eyemouth to Quarrier's orphanage. Effie was so vehement that it was hard for Rosabelle to gainsay her, but she did.

'Effie, I don't want him to go to sea because I can't bear the idea of him being drowned like Dan,' she said flatly.

'When you live lives like ours, you accept these things,' said Effie.

'I can't, I still can't. I never will. Maybe I should take him to London with me.' Rosabelle's eyes were wild.

Grim-faced, Effie stood up and said, 'You're his mother but he hardly knows you. He calls me mother sometimes though I've told him I'm not. Don't take him away. I love him and if he was to go away I'd die. This is his town. Like Jimmy Dip, he'll be an important man here one day.'

'But Jimmy Dip's dead too! How can you wish a death like that on Aaron?'

'I don't wish anything bad on him, but he'd shrivel up and die in a place like London. His destiny is here.'

Rosabelle sank her face into her hands for a moment, but soon looked up again and said in a choking voice, 'We mustn't fight, Effie. I know what he means to you. I love you more than I loved my own mother and I respect you more than any woman I've ever known. He's still a child but let's ask him what he wants to do. If he says his ambition is to go fishing, I'll accept that. If he doesn't, I hope you will.'

Effie stood up. 'I don't think either of us should be the ones to ask him. He'll not know what to say for fear he'll upset us. Alex Burgon'll do it. He's like a grandfather to the lad. I'll go by whatever he finds out, if you will too.'

'I will,' said Rosabelle.

The *Ariel Gazelle* was out at sea for two days and when it docked Effie was waiting on the quayside to speak to Alex, who listened solemnly to her and then nodded.

'I'll do it, and I won't try to influence him. I'll let him speak his mind. He's good at talking to me.'

As usual Aaron went down to the boat that night and helped Alex clean it up because, as always, it needed a thorough scrubbing. As they worked, the old man asked casually, 'You like boats, don't you?'

Aaron looked surprised at what seemed to him a silly question. 'Yes, of course,' he said.

'When you're big, do you want to go to sea?'

'Yes. I want to sail out like you.'

'Have you ever thought of doing anything else?'

'The only other thing I like is whittling wood, but I can do that when I'm not fishing. Besides, my mam – I mean Effie, not my other mother – wants me to go fishing like my father and Jimmy Dip.'

'Would you like to go to London with your real mother?' was the next question.

The child visibly flinched and his face darkened with suspicion. 'I don't want to go to London. I don't really know her. I'd rather stay here with Effie.'

'Don't worry; you won't be made to do anything you don't want to do.'

'When I'm old enough I want to sail with you on the *Ariel Gazelle* and take money home to Effie,' said Aaron.

Burgon looked round his old boat, which was no smarter in appearance than it had been on the day of the storm.

'If it holds together till then,' he said ruefully.

That night he told Effie and Rosabelle what he'd found out. The two women listened in silence, and Rosabelle shook her head as she said, 'It's my own fault. I've stayed away too long.'

'It wasn't easy for you, mourning Dan and everything,' said Effie. They looked at each other, remembering the night Anderson died.

'It's not just that. I'm not good at loving people. I can be fond of them, but I've only ever loved Dan, and when I lost him, I think my heart died too,' said Rosabelle sadly.

'One day you'll get your heart back,' Effie told her, but Rosabelle shook her head as if she knew that would never happen.

When she rose next morning, Rosabelle told Effie, 'I've decided. I'm going back to London. There's no place here for me any more.'

Effie's eyes were full of tears as she said, 'I'll take care of Aaron for you, but there's something I must ask, and please don't think I'm being hard.'

'What is it?'

'If you leave now, I want you to stay away. Don't keep coming back and confusing him. Having you here upsets him. I know he's been worried since you came back because he's been wetting his bed every night – the first time he's done that for years. He's afraid you're going to take him away.'

Rosabelle sobbed. 'I'll do what you want, and I'll still send money, but please keep in touch. I don't want him to forget me completely. I want him to know I'm his mother.'

Effie was crying too. 'Oh, my poor lass, I'll tell him all about you, about how bonny and good and clever you are. Don't worry about that.'

Next day, the train took Rosabelle back to London.

Seven

When Rosabelle reappeared in London without any fore-warning, Rachelle tactfully avoided cross-questioning her about what happened in Eyemouth. If she wanted to talk, she would. If not, it was best to act incurious.

As before, Rosabelle took solace in work and threw herself into a creative frenzy that spread her reputation even wider than it had gone before. The salon was always crowded with fashionable women wanting to buy, and the outworkers were kept stitching all the time.

When she was so busy, Rosabelle found that days, weeks and months swept by, almost unnoticed. Sometimes she found it hard to remember what day it was, or even what season. When she looked out of her studio window and saw the street shrouded in a sulphurous London fog, she shivered and imagined that she could smell the salty scent of the sea.

But when the fog lifted to reveal a beautiful autumn with the trees in the park glowing in jewel-like autumn colours, she was confused to realize that she felt safer when her home was surrounded by blanketing fog.

The yellowish-grey light percolating feebly through her window made her feel she was enclosed in a private place where no one could see her from outside, and she could not see them.

Gradually she sank deeper and deeper into depression, wondering if she'd done the right thing by giving her son away to Effie. Since returning from Eyemouth she had been as engulfed in grief as she was in the first months of her widowhood. She felt helpless, as if her life was ebbing away with nothing happening and nobody caring for her.

Eth caught her weeping one October afternoon. 'What's up, ducks?' she asked, putting a hand on the woman's shaking shoulder.

'I don't know. I'm just tired,' she said.

'You need a holiday. Why don't you go into the country, or back to that town you come from in Scotland? It's a year and more since you were there, isn't it?' Eth suggested.

'I haven't time to take holidays and I wouldn't know where to go . . .'

'Go home and see your family again.'

Tears welled up in Rosabelle's eyes. 'No, I can't . . . I've left my son there, you see. The last time I went back I didn't know him and he didn't know me either . . . I often wonder if I should have stayed in Eyemouth for his sake. I'm a bad mother and I feel such guilt.'

The words poured from her without premeditation, and she was desperate to talk. She wanted Eth to tell her what to do because she felt as if she was wandering alone in an unknown land.

Eth had kind eyes, more understanding than Rachelle's. 'Is your little boy happy? Is he being well treated?' she asked.

'Oh, very happy. He's with his grandmother and he's happier there than he would ever be with me. In fact I don't think he likes me really.' The tears began again.

'He hasn't seen much of you, but that doesn't mean he doesn't like you. Stan hardly ever sees his mother, but he's fascinated by her. If she asked him to jump in the Thames, he'd do it at once. If I ask him to run an errand for me, he grumbles,' said Eth with a laugh. She hugged Rosabelle and said, 'Cheer up, my duck. You're a good girl and a clever one. Me, my sisters – and that includes Sadie – and a lot of other people all depend on you. Do you want me to tell Sadie not to take so many orders? Is she working you too hard?'

'Oh no, don't do that. Work is the only thing that makes me happy.'

Eth hugged her again and said with feeling, 'You poor soul. Any time you want to talk to someone, talk to me.'

Ticked off by Eth, Rachelle tried to shake her partner out of depression by inviting her to a play. 'Come with me to see Pinero's *The Second Mrs Tanqueray*, at the Savoy Theatre tonight. It's meant to be very good,' she said, but Rosabelle refused with an expression that showed she was terrified at the prospect. She went on working all the time, even late at night, while Rachelle was entertaining or out being entertained.

'One day you'll be an old woman and then you'll be sorry you didn't go out enjoying yourself while you could,' Rachelle warned.

I want to enjoy myself. I want to be happy . . . the only problem is I don't know how, thought Rosabelle, but the warning struck a chord of fear in her heart. Outside it was sunny, and for a moment she contemplated putting on the paisley shawl that Rachelle had given her as a birthday gift and taking a turn in the park, but she knew that by the time she walked to the other side of Piccadilly she would be so overcome with panic that she would run all the way back home.

Lying on her work table was one of Effie's weekly letters that arrived regularly, thanking Rosabelle for the money she sent and telling her about Aaron, plus occasional snippets of Eyemouth gossip.

She frowned as she looked at the meaningless scribbles on the page, wishing she could make some sense out of them. Effie's letters were very personal, and though there was now no fear of being charged with Anderson's murder, she resented the fact that she needed someone else to read them to her.

'I must learn to read and write!' she said aloud. But who would teach her? Pride prevented her asking any of the girls in the salon and she knew that Rachelle would make an irritable teacher. What about Eth? She determined to ask her.

'Can you read, Eth?' Rosabelle asked the next time they met.

The answer was cautious. 'Well enough.'

'I can't read at all, or write anything except my name.'

Eth raised her eyebrows and said, 'There's lots of people in the same boat. In fact I'm not much good at the reading either, really.'

Rosabelle's face fell. 'I want to learn. I hoped you might teach me.'

'Not me, love. You need a real tutor,' said Eth.

'Were can I find one?'

'You can find anything if you have the money. D'ye want a man or a woman?'

'A woman, of course,' Rosabelle said and Eth laughed.

'That's a pity. It's a man you need really, but I'll ask around and find someone for you.'

Two days later a sweet-faced, middle-aged woman presented herself at the salon and asked for Miss Rosabelle Scott. She did not look like the type who bought clothes from their establishment, so the assistants told her to wait in the hall while Rosabelle was called.

The stranger's smile transformed her plainness and made her look like an aging cherub. 'My name is Daisy Ashe,' she said, holding out her hand.

Rosabelle smiled back, wondering what this was about, but Daisy took the initiative. 'The cook in the house where I am employed as a governess tells me she heard from a friend of hers that you're looking for a tutor in penmanship. Am I right?'

'Not only penmanship exactly,' said Rosabelle, and to prevent the salon girls from hearing the discussion, she took the stranger up to her work room, and then said, 'I need someone to teach reading and writing.'

'For your children?'

'No, for myself.' Rosabelle's cheeks were flushed but Daisy Ashe was unfazed. 'I would like to do that, and I'll be able to supply references, of course,' she said, pulling a letter out of her shabby reticule. They both looked at it, then at each other, and burst out laughing because, of course, Rosabelle couldn't read it. It was the first time she'd laughed for ages and it made her feel miraculously better.

Daisy said, 'I'm a silly goose, amn't I?' She looked around the room with keen interest and admiration. 'What a lovely room! Are you an artist?'

'No, I design gowns.'

Daisy looked at one of Rosabelle's latest creations draped over a full-busted dressmaker's dummy, and said in admiration, 'If you designed that, I'd say that you're an artist.'

Rosabelle smiled and asked, 'How long do you think it will take to teach me to read and write?'

'I can see that you're intelligent, so not very long. If I come to see you for two hours a week, I'd guess by the end of six months you'd be completely literate. I'm governess to two young ladies in Belgrave Square, which isn't far from here, and I have an afternoon off once a week. I'd come to you then,' said Daisy.

'What do you teach them?' Rosabelle asked.

'French and German mainly. They're finished with ordinary schoolroom subjects and they have other tutors for music and painting.'

'You must be very clever . . . and they are lucky girls.'

'They might not agree with you about that. They can hardly wait to get married and escape from me. The eldest, Felicity, comes out this year and her sister will not be far behind her.' The governess looked sad at that thought.

'What will you do then?'

'I'll have to find another position, or go to live with my brother. He's a parson in Dorset with a family of daughters to educate on a small stipend so he'll be glad of a live-in tutor.' She did not sound happy at the prospect.

Though normally reticent with strangers, Rosabelle was surprised at how comfortable she felt with this dumpy little woman who reminded her so much of Effie. She liked the twinkly brown eyes that made the round face look like that of a kitten; she liked her motherly shape; she liked the interested way she looked at everything, and especially she liked the calm and unsurprised way Daisy took the revelation that her would-be employer was illiterate.

'Please take me as a pupil,' she said and the governess laughed.

'More to the point, will you accept me as your teacher?'

'Of course I will. Can you start tomorrow?' was Rosabelle's next question.

'My day off is Monday. I'll come at half past two if that suits.'

Rosabelle nodded. 'Till Monday then . . . Is it Miss or Mrs Ashe?'

'It's Miss Daisy Ashe. Unfortunately the only gentleman who ever wanted to marry me had no money either.'

'I'll call you Daisy and please call me Rosabelle.'

The lessons went well, but Daisy did not only concentrate on books. She quickly realized how sad and confused her pupil was and made it her business to brighten Rosabelle and try to change her outlook on life.

She started by coaxing her out, suggesting they take the air in Green Park where she calmed the girl's obvious panic by picking up fallen autumn leaves and diverting her by pointing out the trees they came from and telling about their types and differences. In a notebook she carried, she wrote down their names and Rosabelle drew them and copied out the names when she returned home.

Winter came, stripping the branches and chilling the air, so Daisy redirected their walks to Piccadilly, into shops that glittered with decorations for the approach of Christmas. They lingered in the scented warmth, admiring glorious displays by retailers of jewellery, flowers, wine, cigars, hats, furs and leather work.

When she saw Rosabelle's obvious delight at this way of passing the afternoon, Daisy asked, 'I'm surprised you've never done this before. How long have you lived in London?'

'Nine years – no, nearly ten . . .'

'And you've never gone shopping in Bond Street before?'

Rosabelle shook her head. 'No. My partner Rachelle has often asked me to go out with her but I've always refused. If we go out on business, we ride in a cab – Rachelle never walks anywhere and I don't like crowds. I'm scared to go out on my own . . .'

In fact, she was as afraid in the city streets as she would have been in a tiger-infested jungle, and though she knew her fears were irrational that did not make them any less crippling.

There was no official word for the terrors that gripped her, but Daisy was sufficiently sensitive to recognize them and know how to help with gentleness rather than scorn. Also she knew better than to give common sense advice like 'Don't be stupid' or 'Pull yourself together'. Instead she gradually built up her pupil's confidence.

Little by little, Rosabelle literally pulled herself together, mending many of her mental wounds and *almost* her broken heart, but there was still a long way to go.

After her lessons had been going on for three months, she could read a letter from Effie on her own. It was lying on her plate at the breakfast table, and with careful fingers, she opened the envelope to look at the words.

Her heart leapt. Today they made sense! They made words! Without thinking, or whispering the words to herself, she knew what Effie had written. It was like being shown a new and wonderful world.

'I can read! I can read this letter,' she cried out in delight to Rachelle who was moodily drinking coffee beside her.

'Just as well after all the time you've been taking lessons. Tell me what it says. Read it to me,' was the reply.

Rosabelle read the words out, slowly but surely . . . Unfortunately the news it contained was sad.

'Dear Rosabelle . . . Today I have to tell you that my friend Euphen is dying . . . She has a can-ker in her breast . . . I am heartbroken . . . She is my dear-est friend and I will miss her. Aaron and I are well. Love, Effie.'

The next time Daisy came, Rosabelle showed her the letter

and a reply she had drafted. 'Is it right? Have I made any mistakes?' she asked.

Daisy read it. 'Dear Effie, I am very sad to hear about Euphen and know how much you will miss her. She is a good woman. Please give her a kiss from me because I remember how kind she was when I was having Aaron. I am thinking of you all and crying for Euphen . . .' When she had finished reading, Daisy said, 'It is a lovely letter, but I think you should say that you have written it by yourself.'

A sentence was added and the letter was folded, put into its envelope and sent on its way. Daisy was with Rosabelle when Effie's reply came.

> You are a clever girl. I showed Aaron your letter and he admired your penmanship. I thought I'd write a longer letter this time to tell you some of the town gossip now that you can read. Jessie is very thick with Mr Cochrane the minister. They are writing a book but he's the one doing the writing and she's the one that's doing the talking. I think his book will be a good thing because she says he wants to tell the truth about the fishing disaster and what happened after-wards. He is very angry about the meanness of the fund managers – how they let people go hungry when they had all that money in the bank. He says Anderson was a thief but can't say so in the book, though he can hint it. Jessie says he has written a chapter about the boats breaking up on the Hurkars and she told him about you and me watching from the pierhead. He was moved to tears . . .

When she read that last sentence, Rosabelle began to shake and tears cascaded down her cheeks.

'Oh no, oh no,' she sobbed and threw down the letter, covering her eyes with her hands.

Daisy sat appalled, unsure for once how to behave. She lifted up the letter and put a gentle hand on Rosabelle's shaking shoulder as she said, 'What's wrong? Do you want to talk about it?'

The story came tumbling out. Her short, sweet happiness with Dan; the terrible day when he drowned. She told how she watched his death struggles on the cruel rocks and felt herself dying with him.

Daisy wept with her. 'I remember reading about the fishing disaster, but I had no idea you were involved in it,' she said at last.

'Yes, oh yes, me and my mother-in-law Effie who wrote this letter. She lost her husband and three sons all on the same day. My best friend Jessie was going to marry my husband's brother and he died too. We all lost our men,' Rosabelle told her. It was a relief to let it all out.

'That's dreadful, too terrible. And what does she mean about the fund? My brother and I both sent money to help the widows and orphans. It wasn't much, but it was all we could afford at the time,' Daisy told her.

Rosabelle shook her head. 'Thank you,' she whispered brokenly.

'Oh, for heaven's sake, don't thank me. I was very moved by what I read in the newspapers. So many men dying like that . . .'

'Yes. Over a hundred and eighty of them.'

'Did the money people sent help?'

'A little. The widows were given five shillings a week – if they behaved themselves.'

Daisy shook her head in shocked disbelief. 'I'm sure the outside world had no idea what was done with their money. Five shillings a week is so little. What became of the rest?'

Rosabelle shrugged. 'I don't know. People think a lot of it was stolen or frittered away. I don't know the truth.'

Daisy sat stricken, not knowing what to say. 'All you poor women,' she whispered.

Now that she'd started to talk, Rosabelle had to go on. It was the first time she'd told the story right through and coherently, not bit by bit. With her voice cracking she described again watching Dan drown, about giving birth to Aaron and being unable to feel love for him, about being stalked and attacked by Anderson, about hitting him and then seeing his drowned body lying on the paving stones of the harbourside, about running away from Eyemouth because of the terror of discovery, and staying away because of the agony the memory of the place aroused in her. Finally she told Daisy about giving her son away to his grandmother.

Daisy listened, nodding and giving encouragement when Rosabelle showed signs of holding things back. She realized that the girl was undergoing some sort of catharsis, and that it would be best for it all to come out.

'I've never told anyone this before,' Rosabelle said eventually, wiping her eyes. 'Talking about it makes it clearer somehow. I'm beginning to understand. I think I was too close to it before.'

'What do you miss most about your home?' asked Daisy softly.

'Miss about Eyemouth? Nothing really. I hate seeing and hearing the sea. There's more of it than land there and it rules people's lives, sucking them under and then throwing them up again. It's very cruel.'

'But you are from seagoing people, aren't you?'

'Oh yes, on both sides, as far back as anyone knows. Effie keeps telling me that the sea is in our blood. She says my son must go to sea as well because it's his heritage . . .'

'You're afraid of that.'

'Yes.'

'So you do love your son?'

'Do I? I don't know him. He says he wants to go to sea. He loves Effie more than me, he always has. But he's Dan's son and it's my duty to look after him. And he looks so like his father! When I went back, I kept seeing resemblances, the way he moved his head, or pursed his lips. Even the way he walked. How can a child who never saw his father know to walk like that?'

Daisy shook her head. She had her theories about why Rosabelle was staying away from her son, but kept them to herself and hoped that time would solve the problem.

Seeing how very distressed she still was, Daisy took her hand and asked gently, as if she was afraid of a rebuff, 'Do you ever go to church, my dear?'

The answer was a shake of the head. 'Neither of my parents went and neither did Dan. I chose to be married in church, but haven't been in one since. I don't want to go now because if there really is a God, how could he allow something as terrible as the disaster to happen?' said Rosabelle.

'Were you baptized?'

'I don't think so.'

'Would you go to church with me?' asked Daisy.

Rosabelle shook her head doubtfully. 'Why? What good would it do?'

'Let me take you to a service next Sunday,' Daisy suggested and, because Rosabelle did not want to rebuff her too sharply or hurt her feelings, an appointment was made for the following week.

Daisy deliberately chose a church that was only a short walk away from Half Moon Street – St James in Piccadilly, an attractively proportioned red-brick building set behind a tree-filled burying ground with a pointed steeple that had four large clocks set around its base.

When they went inside, Rosabelle was overwhelmed by the size and dignity of the building because it seemed much smaller from outside. To her surprise, a feeling of tranquillity filled her as she stared up at the multi-coloured light streaming in through windows high up above her head.

As they sat waiting for the service to begin, Daisy whispered, 'Isn't it beautiful? Sir Christopher Wren designed it, the same man as built St Paul's.'

Not wishing to appear ignorant, Rosabelle asked, 'In what year?'

'The 1680s, but the steeple didn't go up till 1700.' She indicated dozens of elaborate plaques lining the walls. 'These memorials celebrate famous people – there's one to Lord Palmerston, the old Prime Minister, and another to Emperor Napoleon the Third.'

Rosabelle gazed around, awed and suitably impressed, though neither of those names meant anything to her.

Daisy was still talking softly beside her. 'The choir is magnificent too. Wait till you hear it. It's one of the best in London.'

At that moment, the organ began pealing and an immense feeling of peace filled Rosabelle, taking her out of herself, away from her nervousness and worries. Till then she'd had no idea that music could have such a profound effect on her.

Her whole attitude was different when they emerged from the church into Piccadilly.

'Thank you, Daisy, thank you very much. Will you bring me here again?' she asked.

'Not only will I come back here with you, but I'll take you to other places as well. Next time we could go to St Paul's or even Westminster Abbey,' said Daisy gaily, pleased that her cure seemed to be helping.

Eight

What Effie wrote to Rosabelle about the unexpected friendship between Jessie and Reverend Cochrane was true, and a cause for astonishment and speculation in the town.

Not only did he call frequently at the grocery store, where he leaned over the cheese counter and laughed like a boy at her sallies, but he and she were often seen walking around the cliff tops or through the burying ground in the summer evenings. It was known that the minister was writing a book about the town, but, said the gossips, what was he doing listening to Jessie Johnston? She couldn't even read or write. There must be more to their friendship than that. He must be her lover and the mystery father of little Poppy.

In fact they were just good friends, and he was the first male friend that Jessie ever had who did not try to make love to her, though she recognized that he had a weakness for her but was too gentlemanly and shy to act on it.

She felt as protective towards him as she did towards her little brothers, in spite of the fact that he was almost ten years her senior. Since Rosabelle left she'd had no close friend and he filled that gap. Like many people without formal education, she especially admired his book learning. He had more knowledge than anyone else she'd ever known and it was gratifying to her when he exclaimed with delight when she remembered one of the old stories or legends about the town and told it to him. 'That'll go in the book!' he always cried.

Unfortunately his friendship with a fisher girl did him no good with his congregation, and a member of the kirk session was eventually deputed to question him about his personal life.

The man chosen for this task was Jamie Esslemont, the owner of the corn mill, a worldly person whose own reputation with women was not above reproach.

He called at the manse unexpectedly one evening and, as he and Cochrane sat before the parlour fire, he began, 'You've never been married, have you?'

Cochrane was surprised. He thought everyone knew he was a bachelor. 'No, I'm a bachelor and look likely to remain so. I'm afraid I can't afford a wife on my stipend.'

The miller blinked his sharp eyes and asked, 'Is it only money that's holding you back from marrying? You're not a grieving widower or anything like that?'

'Certainly not.'

'So if we found it possible to make a small increase in your stipend, you might consider marriage? There's a lot of respectable spinsters in the town for you to pick from.'

Cochrane laughed and said, 'I might.' Obviously he was not taking this at all seriously.

'You see that none of the congregation think it would be suitable for you to marry Jessie Johnston, even though she's free? Maybe Mr Stanhope's daughter could be brought back from the south of France to marry you. She'd be a good catch; plenty of money there.'

The minister stopped laughing, appalled at the thought of marrying Hester. 'I'm afraid she wouldn't have me. In fact I'm not all that keen on marrying anyone at the moment.'

'Perhaps if someone pointed out that it might mean you kept your place here, would you think about it then?'

'Good heavens, I don't know. But tell me, am I in danger of losing my church?'

'It's just that people are talking about you and Jessie Johnston. She'd not be suitable for the minister's wife, what with her having two bairns – one Henry Maltman's, right enough, but nobody knows who fathered the second . . . and she's very friendly with you.'

The implications were obvious.

Mixed emotions swept over Cochrane – anxiety first, followed by gratification that he might be considered a possible father for little Poppy, who was the epitome of prettiness and had a sweet nature. She'd never squalled like many babies he'd held at the font – not that Jessie had ever presented either of her daughters for christening.

'Do you think Jessie's baby is mine?' he asked in a guarded tone, but almost preening himself slightly as he looked back at the miller.

'I'm not saying it is, but you know what women are – they're gossiping among themselves and working up the elders to do something about it . . .'

Cochrane straightened up in his chair. 'What will they do?'

'They could ask you to resign. But if you get yourself married to someone else, the whole thing'll be forgotten. It's not that we don't like you . . . it's just that it's not right.'

Cochrane felt a surge of anger, and he was hardly ever angry. 'I had no idea this was such a moral town. Even what I hear about the church elders themselves make me doubt that they are all so narrow minded as to suspect innocent people of misbehaviour . . .'

Esslemont shifted awkwardly in his chair, knowing very well that he was one of the chief offenders. It was common knowledge that, though married, he'd fathered several children by some of the widows of Black Friday. Jessie would know exactly which bairns were his and he wondered if she'd pass on that information to the minister. In fact she already had.

'If the kirk session is considering asking me to resign, they'll have to have better grounds than suspicion, won't they? The paternity of Jessie Johnston's baby is her business, and if anyone says it is mine, I'll defend myself in court,' said Alan Cochrane. To his own confusion he heard his voice squeaking as he justified himself.

The miller withdrew and when he later told his colleagues

about the interview, he said, 'I don't think he *did* father that bairn. He shrieked like a lassie when I accused him of it. He's too much of a nancy for Jessie Johnston.'

Cochrane told Jessie about the interview, but she only laughed and said, 'I hope you told him to mind his own business.'

'But it *is* the session's business. If they think I'm a bad moral influence, they can put me out of my church, and what would I do then?'

'Don't you worry. If they try to put you out of your church because of me, I'll stand up in the kirk and tell them who did father Poppy and that'll stop their tongues.'

'Would you do that?' he asked.

She nodded. 'If I had to, but I hope I don't. I like having a secret. It keeps them all guessing.'

'When I was sitting listening to Esslemont, I realized that I don't want to leave Eyemouth,' said Cochrane sadly.

Jessie put a consoling hand on his arm. 'You won't have to. I've enough on Esslemont to stop his mouth. Anyway, you're part of this town now. I think you should write that book you've been talking about. It might earn you some money and make them see what a clever man you are, and how lucky they are to have you here,' she said.

Her words struck home. *I will write my book. I'll stop thinking about it, and get down to doing it*, Cochrane thought. Throughout the winter months, his shadow was frequently seen through the manse's parlour window, leaning over the desk in the window and scribbling away furiously.

The basis of his book – at least the part about the terrible storm and its aftermath – came from his own journal, which had grown to a prodigious size, a huge pile of closely written pages, but it had to be organized, rewritten and put into chapters. The magnitude of the undertaking at first appalled him, but later, when he was well into it, he enjoyed his task and regretted any time he spent away from his desk.

Jessie encouraged him and took it upon herself, not only to ferret out information for him, but also to keep him working. They continued to go out on their fact-finding walks, and if she was unable to answer his questions she went out of her way to find someone who could.

In fact she became his taskmaster and when she suspected him of idling, or hanging around her cheese counter for too long, she scolded, 'You should be at home writing. When is that book of yours going to be finished? When will people be able to read it?'

With her driving him on, he went back to work, but towards the end his enthusiasm seemed to flag.

She often visited him in his manse, careless of gossiping tongues, and one evening stood on the middle of the study carpet with her hands on her hips as she scolded him. 'You've not finished that book yet, have you? Why not?'

'There's still one or two things I want to find out.' He knew it was a feeble excuse.

'What sort of things? Tell me, and I'll get the answers for you,' she said with a frown.

'About the smuggling trade?' he ventured desperately, and she clicked her tongue.

'I know who could tell you but you don't want to get involved with her. The fake French woman who works with Rosabelle in London must know a lot because she was involved with Tommy Nisbet, the last big smuggler to sail out of here. But as far as I know nobody's been seriously at it since.'

'How can I contact her?' he asked eagerly, for he loved research more than the actual writing.

'You can't. I won't let you. That book's got to be finished without a bit about smuggling or you'll never be allowed to buy another bit of cheese in the shop again.'

'Oh, Jessie, you're a cruel woman,' he groaned and she grinned.

'Yes, I am. And when you've finished, you'll have to put my name inside the cover saying I helped you and kept you at work.'

He laughed. 'I certainly will.' Then his face fell. 'The trouble is, I don't think I'll ever see it in print.'

Jessie stared at him, a look of concern on her face. 'Why not? You're not ill or anything, are you? You don't think you're dying?'

He shook his head. 'It's money. I can't afford to pay to have it printed.'

'But everybody in Eyemouth will buy a copy. You'll make money out of it.'

'If all Eyemouth bought a book, I don't think I'd sell more than three hundred copies and the publisher wants *me* to pay *him* before he'll print it. I've contacted two publishers in Edinburgh, and the best of them said he'll bring it out if I pay half the costs of publication because he doesn't think there'll be enough interest in it to make it financially viable.'

'How much does he want?' asked Jessie, always one to get to the point, especially where money was concerned. She knew Cochrane's stipend depended on the number of people who attended services at his church, and it was never even half full, especially recently, so he lived on very little.

In fact, to make sure he had enough to eat, she often brought him gifts sneaked from the shop – slices of spiced tongue, some of his favourite cheese, a pat of the best butter, a screw of Indian tea, or a bag of broken biscuits – but he needed more than that.

'Hurry up and finish it anyway. I want to see it in print. And I'll do a deal with you. If you finish by Christmas, *I'll* try to get it published,' she said confidently.

He goggled at her. 'How can you? It'll cost a lot of money. Already I've written almost a thousand pages and that costs money to print.'

'A thousand pages, goodness me. No wonder it's taken so long. It'd take most people round here a lifetime to write ten pages, far less a thousand. Finish it, find out the cost and let me know,' she told him.

In fact, his book was finished and lying in his desk. Because he was susceptible to Jessie's bullying – and more to put his own mind at rest than anything else, because he had no real hopes of publication – he parcelled it up and sent it to Edinburgh.

A week later a letter came back telling him the publisher's fee was two hundred pounds. 'That's out of the question, of course,' he said when he told Jessie.

'Maybe not; leave it with me,' said she.

Next day when he called at the shop, she whispered to him, 'I think I've found you a patron. I'll take you to see him tonight.'

'Where are we going?' he asked when she arrived at the manse that evening.

She laughed. 'Ask no questions, just come with me.'

They climbed the hill to the upper town and went along the road that fronted the town's biggest houses. When they reached the gate of Beechwood, Jessie pulled at his sleeve and led him up a path behind the shrubbery to the back premises, warning him to mind his feet as they negotiated potholes and other hazards.

'You obviously know your way around here,' he said as he almost fell into a drain outside the kitchen door.

'I did the washing in their washhouse every night for years, and they don't put on lighting for washerwomen,' she reminded him.

'What are we doing here?'

'Wait and see,' she giggled.

Robert Stanhope was in his library, relaxing deep in a worn leather armchair with a decanter of whisky by his side.

He was obviously expecting his callers. 'Good evening. Would you care for a nip?' he asked with a cordial smile that surprised Cochrane, who had always been in awe of the old man. He suspected that he did not stand very high in his regard, certainly since the 'cauld iron' episode, when he had inadvertently shown his clerical collar to the departing shipping fleet on disaster day. He had not known it was bad luck for a fisherman to see a churchman before setting sail, and that the bad luck could only be averted by the seamen shouting out 'cauld iron'. Dan had been the last man who shouted.

He accepted the offer of a nip of whisky and Jessie disappeared while the men settled down to discuss business.

'I hear you've written a book about the fishing disaster,' said Stanhope.

'Not just the disaster. It's about the town and its history as well. I started making notes about the disaster but got interested in other things too, and I've put them in . . .'

'You minister fellows have nothing else to do but read books and write sermons,' said Stanhope.

Alan made dissenting noises but he needn't have bothered. His opinion was not being asked for. 'I'm told that you say a lot in your book about the disaster fund,' said Stanhope.

'I do.'

'Do you mention my son-in-law, Steven Anderson?'

'Of course.'

'What do you say about him?'

The minister shuffled in his chair. 'I tell the facts as they are known. I don't draw conclusions or give credit to rumours.' He was afraid that Stanhope would forbid publication if Anderson's name was sullied.

'Hmm, I understand your difficulty. There's too many people who were, or might have been, involved. Can I read your manuscript – not all of it because I hear it's huge – just the part about the administration of the fund?'

The answer was a nod. He had nothing to lose. *I've wasted my time coming here*, he thought. *All he wants to do is edit my writing and make sure I don't besmirch his family.*

'I'll bring it to you tomorrow,' he said, rising to his feet.

'Finish your drink before you rush off, man,' said Stanhope.

Cochrane swallowed the whisky and looked around for Jessie but she had disappeared. 'I'll be off then,' he said.

Stanhope rose too. 'Let me show you out. This time, use the front door. It's much more suitable for a minister than creeping in through the back,' he said with a laugh.

A week passed – a week of depression for Cochrane, who was convinced that his book would never be published, and not only that, but his congregation was dwindling so fast that even if he was not asked to resign, there might soon be no one left for him to preach to.

He was on the point of writing to boys' schools enquiring about a master's position when Jessie ran out of the shop and waved to catch his interest as he walked past one morning.

'Write and tell that publisher that you have the money and he can go ahead and print your book,' she said in a voice full of glee.

He stared at her in disbelief. 'I have two hundred pounds?' he asked.

'Mr Stanhope says he'll pay. He likes your book. Come in and he'll tell you himself.' It was true. 'I was most impressed by what you've written. Your book is a testimonial to the people of Eyemouth,' Stanhope said when he walked into the office.

'You don't mind what I said about the disaster fund?'

'You've been very unspecific, but you don't leave the reader in any doubt that it's been mishandled in more ways than one. Not that I can do anything now because it's out of my hands – out of everybody's hands really. I don't like committees and the disaster one was too big, too scared and too prejudiced. But I'm glad some things have been brought out,' said Stanhope.

'Are you really prepared to pay for publication?' asked Cochrane.

'Yes.'

'I feel very guilty about taking so much money from you,' he protested, but Stanhope cut him off with a wave of the hand.

'It's a business proposition. Pay it back when people buy the book,' he told him.

'But what if it doesn't sell?'

'Don't be a pessimist. We can use the unsold copies to light our fires. At a thousand pages per copy, they'll give a lot of heat.'

Was Stanhope making a joke? Cochrane was not sure, but smiled anyway.

Later that night he was waiting for Jessie as she left the shop after work, and stepped along beside her. 'I want to thank you, but I'm worried in case the book doesn't sell and Mr Stanhope loses his money.'

She shrugged. 'He can afford it, and he wants people to know what happened here. He was as angry as you at the way the fund money was distributed, but couldn't say so for several reasons – most of the trustees' families are his customers, and Anderson married his daughter. The book'll sell, I'm sure of it, and more than that, it'll tell what this town was like before and after the storm. It'll be a good thing if the outside world knows that Eyemouth survived in spite of everything.'

He looked at her with surprise. 'I didn't know you felt so strongly about it,' he said.

'There's a lot of things nobody knows about me,' she said sharply.

When Jessie told Effie that Cochrane's book was being published, the other woman's eyes lit up and she said, 'That's very good,' but suddenly her expression changed. 'I hope he doesn't make it all holy and God-fearing like most ministers' books. We're not that sort.'

'He's been here long enough to know that. From what he's told me he's put in all the details of the big storm, all the men's names and the names of their boats, and he's also written a history of the town, right back to the time of Queen Elizabeth, whoever she was,' said Jessie.

'Folk'll read it,' said Effie.

Jessie leaned towards her and said, 'Especially when they find out that he doesn't let the relief committee off lightly. He as good as says that Anderson fiddled the money. And to think it started off at over fifty thousand pounds!'

'Oh aye, they'll want to read that,' said Effie with satisfaction.

In her turn, she hurried off to tell the news to her friend

Euphen, though she found it sad to go to Burgon's home nowadays because Euphen was very ill and now bedridden. The cancer that riddled her body was eating her away, and she was skeletally thin, but her sweetness and faith in God were undiminished.

Euphen had been dozing, but opened her eyes and brightened when she saw her friend by her bed.

'Is everything all right with you, Effie? How's Aaron?' she whispered.

'We're fine, but what about you? How's the pain?'

'Not too bad today. Poor Alex's been brewing me up potions to make me sleep, and William's wife has moved in to take care of me. She's a gentle, kind lassie.'

It would be tactless, Effie thought, to show grief before her dying friend, so she tightened her lips to stop them trembling and said, 'I've brought you some news. Cochrane's finished his book and it's gone to the printer's. Jessie says it'll be in the shops next month. I'll get a copy and bring it to you.'

Euphen smiled. 'I like Mr Cochrane, but I never thought he was much good as a minister. Maybe he's better as a book writer. I hope I'm strong enough to read it.'

'I'll read it to you if you're not,' Effie said

Unfortunately Euphen died two days before the book was published. The day after the funeral, Effie bought a copy, and when she held its hard blue cover in her hands, she wept in memory of her friend.

When he came back from school, Aaron saw her poring over the thick tome and asked what it was. She held the open copy out to him and said, 'That page tells about my husband and your father and his brothers. Read it for yourself.'

He took the book in both hands and bent his head over it. His reading was fluent and he finished quickly. When he looked up at her, his face was shocked. 'Is that true? Is what he says right?'

'What bit are you asking about? You've heard the story often enough.'

'But you never told me that my father died on the Hurkars, and no one could get to him.'

'Yes, that's true.'

'And that my London mother saw it happening?' He always referred to Rosabelle as his 'London mother'.

Effie managed to say, 'Yes, she did.'

'How old was she?'

'Nineteen.'

'Oh my God, no wonder she ran away,' he said and closed the book.

The History of Eyemouth and the Fishing Disaster made a minor sensation. The review in the *Scotsman* praised it highly and called it 'a sensitive and heart-rending work'. Sales far exceeded expectations, and Cochrane managed to pay Stanhope back within three months. Not only that, but his standing with his congregation rose enormously.

He even made several hundred pounds for himself and wished that his mother had been alive to know about his success, but she'd died the previous year.

Jessie was delighted. 'It's made our town famous – and for a good reason this time. Now you'll have to write something else,' she told him.

He groaned. 'It's taken nearly sixteen years to write this. I can't face doing it again.'

But in fact he was secretly considering another project – a history of Berwickshire, which would be an even bigger undertaking. It would probably take him the rest of his life.

Nine

On a fine evening in 1899, Effie stood on the end of the pier and stared out at the heaving sea, thinking about her dead husband and children. Though she never believed it possible, her raging agony of loss had softened into a melancholy that she now cherished rather than feared.

A hand touched her shoulder and she turned to see Jessie beside her.

'You're looking very sad, staring out at the sea like that,' said the young woman, slipping her arm through Effie's.

'I was thinking about Jimmy and the boys, wondering what they'd be like if they were alive today.'

Jessie nodded. 'I often think about Henry, but it's hard to remember what he looked like. I feel bad about that sometimes . . .'

Effie patted her hand. 'Don't. You've done well. It's people like you who're bringing life back to this town. Bit by bit it's recovering. It'll never forget the disaster and the men who died, and in a hundred years' time, I hope people here will be shedding tears for them, but life goes on. Live your life, Jessie. I'm proud that my Henry had the sense to pick you out and bring you into my family. I don't know what I'd do without you.'

Jessie's eyes filled with tears and she wiped them away with the back of her hand. 'It's you the town's proud of, you and women like you who gave us the spirit to fight. It would've been easy to go to the drink like my mother, or jump into the sea like Rosabelle's, but you kept on fighting. I want to be like you when I'm your age.'

'I'm proud of my town. I'm proud of the way the people go on fighting. I want them to keep on fishing . . . that's why I'm watching for the *Ariel Gazelle*. Alex took Aaron out with him this morning for his first fishing trip. They'll be back before the tide turns.'

'Aaron's going to the fishing?' Jessie asked in a doubtful voice. She knew Rosabelle would not want that.

Effie gave her a defiant glance. 'He wants to. Alex offered him a place and he said he wanted to go.'

'You're sure he's not going because he doesn't want to disappoint you? He knows how proud you are of Jimmy Dip. Maybe he wants to be like him.'

'Jimmy Dip's got nothing to do with it,' said Effie sharply. 'If Eyemouth is ever going to be a big port again, our young men have to go to sea. Black Friday was a freak. There'll probably never be another storm like it.'

'Let's hope not,' said Jessie as she raised her eyes to scan the horizon. Her sight was sharper than Effie's nowadays and she was the first to spot the boats coming over the horizon. 'Here they come! Is that the *Ariel Gazelle* in front? Yes, I think it is. He's back, Effie. He's safe this time.'

As Aaron climbed up to the harbour wall, he saw his grandmother waiting for him with a big smile on her face.

'How did it go?' she asked as her eyes delighted in her grandson's handsomeness. At seventeen he still had a strong look of Dan, but there were differences now because his hair was not as jet black as his father's. In fact, in certain lights it looked red, and she hoped that when his beard came through, it too would be red. Then he'd look like a pirate.

His shoulders were not as broad as Dan's either, for he had more of Rosabelle's lean elegance, and he'd inherited her long hands, not the Maltman family's short stubby fingers.

He grinned at her. 'Good. It went well.'

Her old friend Alex came up the ladder behind him and also smiled. 'You can be proud of him. He did a good job. He pulled his weight, and didn't take any chances.'

'I am proud, indeed I am,' she said and gave the boy a

nudge. 'Come on home, Aaron, I've a fine supper waiting for you.'

As he ate, she talked about his future.

'I heard today that one of the Purveses is having a new boat built. I've asked if you could buy a share. Purves is thinking about it.'

This was a surprise to Aaron, and he looked up with doubt clearly showing on his face.

'Which Purves?' he asked.

'Big Tom. He's a good seaman. If you put in a hundred pounds, you could have one quarter of the boat.'

'What's it called?'

'The *Three Sisters*. His father had one with the same name. And don't worry, it didn't go down in the storm.'

Aaron pulled a face. 'I'd rather sail with Alex, Mam.' Though he was almost grown up, he still called her 'Mam' and thought of her as his mother, though he knew very well that Rosabelle, in London, was the source of all their material comforts.

'But Alex'll be giving up soon. He's sixty and his rheumatics are bad. The *Ariel* is just about ready to be scrapped. You must get a place on a good boat and carry on Jimmy Dip's tradition.'

He frowned. Secretly he felt burdened by his grandmother's expectations for him. He'd grown up with her stories about Jimmy Dip – the best seaman of them all, according to her. If he was so good, Aaron privately wondered, why did his boat founder? But he would never dare to ask that question.

When he cleaned his plate, he stood up and said, 'I think I'll go along to Jessie's to tell her and the girls about my first trip out.'

He'd spent much of his growing up years with Jessie's daughters and they were his closest friends. Their mother too was the person he loved best in the world after Effie. He enjoyed her cheeky irreverence; and the flirtatiousness which had become such a part of her that she could not resist turning it on every man she came across – even him. By now it was more a habit than serious, for Jessie was turning into a matron, her rackety past behind her.

Effie approved of Aaron's attachment to Jessie and the girls. In her heart she cherished the hope that he might marry tomboyish Poppy, who was growing into a slightly less boisterous version of her mother.

If only I knew who fathered that bairn, she thought to herself, but Jessie was still as closed as a clam on the subject.

Henry's child, Henrietta, was quieter, and not as obviously pretty as her sister.

'How old is Poppy now?' Effie asked in the light way that showed she had an ulterior motive.

'You know as well as me. She's twelve,' he said.

'In a few years all the lads in the district will be after her,' said Effie.

'Her mother will sort them out,' he replied with a grin. 'She won't let Poppy marry anyone who doesn't come up to her standards.'

Effie nodded. 'That's true. She's certainly had enough practice summing up men. I've always thought that you and Poppy would be a good match.'

He laughed again, but said nothing.

Next day he was helping Alex Burgon sluice down the decks of his boat when a small boy went pelting up the harbour and hammered on Effie's door.

Aaron knew she was out, visiting a sick friend in the upper town, and called, 'She's not in. What do you want?'

'Jessie from the shop sent me. She wants Effie to go there right away. Old Stanhope's died.'

Aaron and Alex looked at each other in surprise, but wiped their hands and climbed out of the boat to follow the boy to Stanhope's shop.

There was a crowd of people outside the closed front door, but Aaron, who knew the shop well from illicit visits to Jessie over the years, said, 'Let's go round the back to the yard. We can get in that way.'

Inside the vast back premises, people stood around looking shocked but there was no sign of Jessie.

When Aaron asked where she was, a woman in a white apron pointed to the office. 'She's in there with him. She was there when he died.'

Jessie, weeping, was sitting on the floor beside the long body of her employer. His face was covered with a white apron, carefully folded.

She looked up and sobbed. 'Oh, Aaron, where's your mam?'

'She'll be here soon.' He had no doubt that the news would reach Effie quickly.

'What happened?' asked Alex, bending down and putting out a hand to help Jessie up.

'I took him his morning sherry as usual. He said he was feeling tired so I told him to drink it up and went to get him another. When I put it on his desk, he reached out his hand like this –' she extended her arm – 'and gave a sort of groan, put his other hand on his chest, and just fell forward.'

He looked at her in sympathy. 'What a fright you must have got,' said Aaron.

She stared back at him with swollen eyes. 'I was that fond of him. He was a good, kind man to me.'

Alex looked around and asked, 'Has someone fetched the doctor?'

'Aye, he's been. It was an apoplectic fit. Instant, he said. He's gone to fetch the undertaker.'

'Come on, Jessie, let me take you home,' said Aaron gently, and he led her away through the back to avoid the curious onlookers in front of the shop. They were halfway home when they met Effie running up from fishing town.

'I've just heard about old Mr Stanhope. Is it true he's dead?' she asked Jessie, who burst into noisy tears.

'She's shocked. She was with him when he died,' Aaron explained, not quite sure what to do because Jessie was holding on to him with both hands and weeping on his shoulder.

91

'Away back to the boat and help Alex. I'll take her home,' said Effie and took over from him.

When he went home that night for supper, Effie was alone, banging about in the kitchen with what seemed like more noise than usual. He sat down at the table and asked, 'How's Jessie?'

'She's better. Henrietta's looking after her.' Jessie's eldest daughter helped out with the infant class in the town school because she wanted to be a teacher.

'And Mr Stanhope?'

'They took him up to Beechwood and sent for his son. He's coming down tonight.'

Aaron wondered why his grandmother was so grim-faced. She had not been close to Stanhope, so perhaps she was upset because someone who was almost a contemporary had died suddenly.

'How old was he?' he asked.

'Older than me. About seventy, I think.'

So it wasn't that. 'It's a sad business,' he ventured.

She turned round quickly to say, 'Is it? It's a very funny business if you ask me.'

She's angry. Why is she angry? he wondered, but no matter how many other questions he asked, she would not say any more about the business.

Everard was in Beechwood by nightfall. The shop was closed and Alan Cochrane was summoned to discuss funeral arrangements. Finally a telegram was sent to Menton to summon Hester, who had not been back for ten years. She and Louisa set out at once and were in Eyemouth two days after her father died.

Jessie stayed in her own house and did not answer the door to curious callers. Effie furiously banged pots and pans together on her kitchen range and snapped answers to her grandson's attempts at conversation.

As a sign of respect, all the shops in the town closed down on the afternoon of the funeral. Even the fishing boats stayed at home. In his capacity as the biggest chandler in the district, Stanhope had dealt with all the skippers for fifty years.

He was buried with much pomp and ceremony, and after he was laid in his grave, his family and friends gathered at Beechwood for what was discreetly referred to as 'a refreshment'. Some of them forgot the solemnity of the occasion and had to be gently persuaded to go home at nightfall.

Then Robert Stanhope's children, his sister, his nieces and nephews gathered in his library for the serious business of hearing about their legacies and inheritances

The town lawyer looked solemn as he propped his pince-nez on the bridge of his nose and peered at them all. 'There are a few surprises in this will, I'm afraid,' he said.

'Please proceed. I don't think my father had any dark secrets,' said Hester in an attempt at lightness. She had become quite foreign-looking after her years of living abroad, and, like Rachelle, affected a French accent.

Her daughter Louisa, a timid-looking girl who had inherited Anderson's abundant brown hair and heavy jaw, sat beside her mother with downcast eyes. When introduced to well-wishers after the funeral she'd said nothing except, '*Bonjour.*' Many mourners wondered if she could actually speak English.

The lawyer looked around at the party, grimaced anxiously and said, 'Before I can begin with the reading, I think it is only correct that his widow is brought in.'

Hester sat bolt upright in her chair and let out a shriek. 'His widow! What widow? My mother has been dead for twenty-five years.'

The lawyer ignored this, looked across at Everard and asked, 'Will you fetch the lady, please?'

Everard rose and left the room, while Hester babbled, turning in her chair and speaking to the others. 'What sort of nonsense is this?' They shrugged and looked dumbfounded. It was obviously a surprise to them too, but they did not have to wonder long.

The heavy library door swung open. Everard stepped inside

and held on to the handle while he ushered someone in. When she saw who it was Hester stood up and let out a banshee shriek. 'Never!'

The newcomer was Jessie. Discreetly dressed in a dark grey gown, she stepped into the room and let Everard guide her towards an empty chair.

'This is impossible. Tell me it's impossible!' Hester called out and subsided into her chair, fanning herself with a handkerchief before slumping into what looked like a faint.

Her brother walked across to a banquette and poured a measure of brandy into a glass which he took across to her. 'Drink that. You're going to need it,' he said grimly.

She sat up and drank the brandy. When she seemed more in control of herself, the lawyer asked, 'Can I proceed?'

Everard nodded. Jessie said nothing but sat with her head down and eyes fixed on the floor so no one could tell what she was thinking.

Robert Stanhope's last will and testament was very straight forward.

'To my only son, Everard, the sum of two thousand pounds and all my stocks and shares,' the lawyer read.

This brought Hester to her senses. 'All?' she asked.

'All,' agreed the lawyer.

'Please go on,' said Everard.

The lawyer continued, 'To my *eldest* daughter, Hester –' there was a pause during which Hester could be heard gasping as if in the grip of an attack of palpitations – 'the sum of one thousand pounds and my chandlery business, which she would be well advised to sell because she knows nothing about it. It should fetch a good sum. To her daughter Louisa I leave five hundred pounds.'

Hester opened her mouth to speak but the lawyer went on. 'There's more. I hope Hester considers this a generous bequest under the circumstances.'

'But what about the grocery store and this house? And why do I only get one thousand and Everard gets two?' she asked.

Her brother spoke up now. 'Because Father paid the missing money back into the relief fund after your husband drowned, and sent money to your husband's mother and sister till they both died,' he said.

She fell silent, her face set in a tight mask. Turning to her daughter, she said sharply, 'Leave the room, Louisa. You should not be hearing this.' Louisa left.

The lawyer looked at Jessie and cleared his throat before he continued. 'I will go on. To my wife, Jessie, I bequeath my licensed grocery business in its entirety, lock, stock and barrel. To my youngest daughter, Poppy Johnston, I bequeath Beechwood House, with all its contents, on condition she changes her name to Poppy Stanhope.'

Hester stood up, stumbled, fell into an undignified heap on the carpet and had to be calmed with more brandy.

'Poppy! That baby she was carrying was *his*? You whore!' she screamed at Jessie, who shrugged.

'If you drink any more brandy you'll do yourself an injury,' Jessie rejoined.

Hester, still on the floor, switched her gaze to Everard and accused him in turn. 'You knew about this, didn't you? Are you sleeping with her as well? He must have been mad. I don't believe that Poppy is his child. I'll contest the will.'

'Don't bother. It's all true. He told me about the baby and his marriage after you left home – and no, I don't sleep with my stepmother,' Everard told his sister.

'But you did nothing? You could have had the old fool certified insane. There must have been something wrong or he'd have made the marriage public. If it was above board he'd have taken her into his house and given her his name.' She stared at Jessie for a moment, then sneered. 'Oh, I forgot. Fishwives don't change their names when they marry, do they?'

Cheeks blazing, Jessie retaliated. 'He was far from insane! I have papers to prove we were married and he acknowledged Poppy before a notary. Ask your lawyer if you don't believe me. He asked me to live with him, but I didn't want that. We made a bargain. I like my freedom and I wasn't ready to settle down, and only married him because I was carrying his baby. He wanted to make sure that it got its share of his estate. Poor soul, he was delighted to be a father again at his age.'

'Pschaw! You mean *you* wanted a share of his estate. Well, don't count on it because I'll drag you through the courts and prove you forced him to leave you the shop.' Hester was beside herself with fury.

Embarrassed by the row, one by one the other relatives slunk away, not waiting to hear what minor legacies had been left to them.

As they left the library, they heard Hester shrieking at her brother, 'How could you keep such a secret? How could you allow our father to be led astray by that trollop who's never been any better than a *prostitute*? I know her reputation and always suspected she was up to no good with him, but he wouldn't listen, taking her into the shop and giving her things, don't think I didn't notice. But he can't have married her legally without anyone in this town knowing. It's not possible.'

Sighing, Everard put out a hand and hauled his sister off the floor. 'Get up. The marriage is quite legal. They did it at Lamberton Toll. He was cock-a-hoop about that.'

Hester threw back her head and howled, 'My God, I don't believe it! I don't believe any of this. I don't believe my father ran away to a tollhouse and married a tart. I don't believe he fathered her child. He must have been insane.'

Everard's patience snapped. 'Stop saying that. He wasn't in the least insane. You'll be well advised to accept what he's left you and make no more fuss. As a lawyer I know that if Jessie was to contest the will, she might get even more than she has at the moment.'

Jessie was standing by the fireplace, staring at them. She shook her head and said, 'I'm content. I won't be going to any court. I didn't marry him for his money. I did it to please him at first but I came to love him, really love him, and I miss him sore.' Tears began to run down her cheeks.

Brother and sister stared at her, Everard silenced by her obvious sincerity, Hester still mad with anger. 'You say you're content. No wonder! You've been left a thriving business – one of the best in the whole district – and this house as well. No wonder you're content,' she shrieked.

'Please restrain yourself. The servants will hear you,' Everard said anxiously but he was wasting his breath.

She went on and on. 'You are a whore and a thief. That's what you are!'

Jessie wiped her eyes and said with a return of her old spirit, 'Robert knew you'd take on something terrible when you found out. I think he liked the idea.'

'Robert? Do you call my father Robert?'

'Well, he was my husband,' snapped Jessie, 'and this is my daughter's house now. We'd be obliged if you and your daughter move out as soon as possible. I'll move in here in three days' time and if you're not away, I'll take a broom to you.'

Ten

'I am mad at Jessie. To think that she married old Mr Stanhope and never let on to anybody. I asked her time and time again who Poppy's father was but she just laughed. I'm hurt that she didn't trust me. I'm her mother-in-law after all – or nearly her mother-in-law – and I thought I knew everything about her. She's a dark horse and no mistake.'

Effie's indignation made holes in the writing paper where her pen had jabbed.

When she read the letter Rosabelle laughed. 'Good for Jessie,' she said aloud.

Rachelle was sitting on the other side of the room studying fashion plates. 'Is that the girl who saw you off at Berwick station? Small and dark with a sparkle in her eye?'

'Yes, that's her.'

'What's she done?'

'Married well, that's all.'

'I told you she'd make good.'

'Yes, you did. I've always thought that you and she are alike – not in looks but in character. You both know what you want and go out to get it,' Rosabelle said.

'That's the only way to live, but who did she marry?'

'A rich man called Stanhope who's just died and left her his grocery store and a big house,' said Rosabelle.

'Clever girl. You should ask her for lessons,' said Rachelle. Rosabelle flushed and went back to reading her letter. She was irritated because recently Rachelle had started being very cutting and sarcastic, not caring what she said. Not only was she condescending to Rosabelle but she was high-handed and rude with the customers too, and Rosabelle did not like that.

Their summer collection was as good as previous years, but some customers drifted away to other *modistes* because Rachelle insisted on raising their prices to an exorbitant level.

'You can't ask people to pay so much for ordinary things like this,' Rosabelle protested, holding up a tea gown of flimsy muslin for which Rachelle demanded a hundred guineas.

'Of course I can. If they went to Paris it would cost them far more.'

'But this isn't Paris, it's Half Moon Street, and that gown cost us less than a pound to make.'

Rachelle pouted. 'I set the prices and I've told you before that we must ask for as much as we can get. That's the only way they respect us.'

Rosabelle sensed that Rachelle was losing interest in the business, and the prospect of being left to cope alone filled her with fear. She could never run the social side of the enterprise, far less find suppliers and haggle with them as Rachelle did – or used to do. Her role was to stay in the background and produce the designs. That was crucial, she knew, but she needed a partner to promote her work.

Pondering this problem, she was staring out of the studio window after her discussion of prices with Rachelle when she saw Eth walking up the street carrying a parcel, and hurried downstairs to see the latest piece.

But when the parcel was opened, a dress emerged that made them look at each other in disappointment. Rosabelle said, 'Dull, isn't it?'

'It's not my fault,' protested Eth.

'I know. And it's not mine either. It's that material. It looks cheap.' The dress was made of undistinguished pale blue taffeta.

'It is cheap. Who's it for?' Eth asked, and Rosabelle told her it was an order for the youngest daughter of one their richest and most discriminating clients.

'This won't please her, especially if she's out to catch a rich husband for the girl. What's up? Are you two going bust?' asked Eth anxiously.

'I don't think so, though I don't handle the money. Rachelle does all that. I do know she's still charging huge prices for the things we make.'

'Not for long if this is anything to go by,' said Eth gloomily.

'The design's good. We ought to make it again out of better material,' Rosabelle decided.

'You'd better ask *her* first,' said Eth, nodding in the direction of Rachelle's office.

When they took the disappointing dress in to show Rachelle, she lifted one of the ribbons that drifted from its waist and said dismissively, 'Not one of your best efforts, I'm afraid.'

Rosabelle bridled and snapped, 'Don't blame me. It's because you bought cheap material for it, but there's time to do it again if you go out now and buy something better.'

Rachelle turned and drifted out of the room. 'I can't be bothered,' she called back over her shoulder.

'What's wrong with her? Is she sick?' asked Eth, looking at Rosabelle.

'I don't know. She's been odd lately. It's as if she's in a dream half the time. She's rude to everybody and she's stopped paying any attention to my work, and now it seems that she is buying the first thing that comes to hand. Sometimes she doesn't even get out of bed till the afternoon.'

'What's she taking?'

'Taking? Do you mean medicines?'

'Not really. Is she taking laudanum?'

Rosabelle's face showed horror. 'Laudanum? I don't think so. Why should she?'

'She used to take it, but she stopped after she had Stan. It made her useless,' said Eth.

'Will you ask her if she's taking it again? You're her sister. I wouldn't know how to bring up the subject,' said Rosabelle, who had only ever heard of laudanum as a medicine for ladies with the vapours – not an ailment that bothered Eyemouth women much.

'I'll try,' said Eth, 'but she's as big a liar with me as she is with you.'

That afternoon, Daisy came to give Rosabelle more bad news.

'I'm afraid I'll have to stop giving you lessons, but you're reading well now so you don't really need me any more.'

'But you can't leave me! You're my friend. I'd never go out without you . . . Why are you giving me up?'

'My employer has given me notice and I'm leaving Belgrave Square next week. The girls don't need a governess any more because they're both getting married soon. I'll miss you too but I have to go.' Daisy's face was very sad.

'Where to?'

'Dorset, I'm afraid.'

'Dorset?' To Rosabelle it sounded as far away as the moon. 'You can't go. You must stay here. I know what I'll do. I'll hire you to do some of the work Rachelle's always done. She's not very well and needs help.'

'My dear, I can't bully customers around the way Rachelle does.'

'I'm not expecting you to do that. You can write up the bills, and send out our letters, that sort of thing. You'd be wonderful at it. We really need you because things are getting out of hand.'

So Daisy was hired and proved to be an asset, taking so much work off Rachelle's shoulders that even she curbed her tongue and was polite in the new employee's presence.

Daisy was installed in Rachelle's office and given a bedroom in the attic. She and Rosabelle continued their friendly outings to shop, going to the park, and visiting churches round about. On one of their expeditions, Daisy said, 'I don't think Madame Rachelle is quite herself at the moment.'

'I know. She's been acting strangely for some time. What's your opinion?' Rosabelle asked.

'I'm worried because she won't pay the bills and there's a lot of them outstanding.'

Rosabelle sighed. 'Oh dear, that's another worry. I'll have a word with her.'

Rachelle dismissed the bill problem lightly. 'I'll pay them tomorrow,' she said.

But she didn't, and Daisy again complained. 'Our suppliers and tradesmen are very annoyed. They ought to be paid soon,' she said.

Rosabelle groaned. 'Give me the bills. I'll pay them out of my own funds,' she said. Daisy shook her head. 'I think there's something very wrong with Rachelle. Does she take laudanum?' she asked flatly.

'Her sister Eth asked me that as well. I don't know. Eth said she used to, long ago, but stopped, and she asked Rachelle about it but Rachelle said she's only tired because of over-work.'

Daisy shook her head. 'There's more to it than that, I'm afraid. One of the ladies I used to work for was addicted to opium, and she behaved exactly like Madame Rachelle.'

'Opium?' Rosabelle was horrified.

'That's what laudanum is, my dear; it's opium mixed with quinine. People take it medicinally in small doses – only a quarter ounce a day usually, but sometimes they go on till they're up to three or four ounces. If they keep increasing the dose, it can kill them. Is there any way we can find out if she's taking it – and how much?'

Though it was afternoon, Rachelle was still asleep when Rosabelle knocked on her bedroom door. When there was no reply, she went in and asked the curled-up figure on the bed, 'Are you all right? It's half past one.'

A groan was the response and Rachelle sat up, pushing hair back from her haggard face. The room smelled stale and she looked very old indeed.

'Did you say half past one? The middle of the night?' she asked.

'No, midday.'

'I've slept for fifteen hours. I must have needed it.'

'You've slept longer than that. I heard you going upstairs at eight last night.'

On a table by the bedside there was a blue glass flask and a tumbler which Rachelle ineffectually tried to lift. Seeing Rosabelle's eyes on her, she stopped and grumbled, 'Don't stare at me like that. Go away. You're worse than those awful women who guard apartments in Paris.'

'I think you're ill. Will I fetch a doctor?'

'Of course not. I'm not ill. I'm overtired, I told Daisy that when she was going on about the bills. I have to carry the responsibility of this business on my shoulders while all you do is sit and draw.'

'You're not carrying it very well because the bills haven't been paid for weeks and some people are refusing to deal with us.' For once Rosabelle stood her ground, staring Rachelle out.

There was no answer and Rachelle's hands were shaking so badly that she could not pull the glass stopper out of the flask neck, so Rosabelle took it from her and asked, 'What's this you're taking?'

'It's medicine.'

'I thought you said that you're not ill. What is it for?'

'It makes me sleep.'

'But you don't need that. You've been sleeping for hours.' Rosabelle sniffed at the neck of the bottle and said, 'It's laudanum, isn't it? How much are you taking?'

'What business is it of yours?'

'It's very much my business. If you go on like this, you'll ruin us. I'm fetching a doctor for you whether you want one or not.' And Rosabelle stormed out of the room, forgetting her usual temerity because she sensed that this was very serious and could spell their downfall.

Wonderful Daisy, who seemed to know everything, was consulted and recommended a doctor who'd successfully treated her laudanum-addicted ex-employer.

'He's most successful and very discreet, though his fees

are high. People say he's even been called in to treat the Queen herself,' she told Rosabelle.

'Does the Queen take laudanum?' Rosabelle asked in surprise.

Daisy only shrugged and said, 'So I've heard.'

'I don't suppose it matters who he sees or what he charges. Rachelle needs help. What's his address?'

'He's in Savile Row, quite near. I'll send one of the maids to fetch him,' said Daisy.

Rosabelle expected a professorial-looking grey beard, and was surprised when a dapper man in his early forties arrived an hour later. His tailcoat was well cut and he wore an exotic-looking flower in his buttonhole.

When she caught a whiff of tobacco from him, she recoiled, remembering Anderson, and her manner became very formal, even hostile, as she greeted him.

He introduced himself by saying, 'I'm Dr Worthing. You sent for me, madam?'

'Not for myself. I've called you in because my business partner is ill. We think she's been dosing herself with laudanum. Rather too much of it, I'm afraid,' she said stiffly.

He nodded as he handed his shiny silk hat and walking stick to the housemaid. The only other person Rosabelle had ever seen who wore such beautiful hats was Tommy Nisbet. *Rachelle will like this fellow*, she thought.

'Where is the patient?' he asked.

'In her bedroom on the first floor. I'll take you there.' As she led the way up the sweeping staircase, he walked behind, admiring her tall, slim figure and the glimpse of elegant ankle that showed beneath the hem of her skirt. The mass of golden, tightly curled hair piled up on her head gave her the look of a Greek goddess, but, like a statue, she was as chilly as marble.

Haughtily she opened a door and gestured for him to go in. 'I'll wait downstairs,' she said.

He stepped into a room that resembled a high-class bordello, with lavishly looped curtains, long, ornately framed mirrors and two chaise longues covered in shiny scarlet tapestry. A woman with dyed black hair and a thickly painted face lay on the one nearest the fireplace.

He pulled up a chair to face her and, assuming his professional tone, said briskly, 'I'm Dr Worthing and I hear you've not been well. Your friend downstairs is worried about you.'

'Rosabelle fusses too much.' The woman's accent sounded foreign, but was difficult to place.

He decided to get straight to the point. 'Have you been doping?' he asked.

'What do you mean?'

He ignored that question because he knew the answer perfectly well. Instead he asked her another. 'It's opium, isn't it? How much are you taking?'

To his surprise, she said flatly, 'Four ounces.'

'A day? In quinine?'

'Yes.'

'It'll be difficult to cut that down quickly, but it can be done, providing you want to. Stopping takes time and willpower.'

She sighed, lifting her shoulders expressively, and said, '*C'est bien.* I'm not short of willpower.'

She's pretending to be French, but not very successfully, he registered.

'How long have you been taking it?' he wanted to know.

'I first started years ago but stopped for a long time. But people say you always go back in the end, don't they? A friend used to bring supplies from France, but he drowned. Now I buy it from people at the docks. My son fetches it for me.'

'It's an expensive habit,' he said.

'It is, but fortunately I can afford it,' she agreed.

He looked round the room wondering again if she was a high-class madam, for she was very expensively dressed and the furnishings lavish. He'd only seen women in the rest of the house, but the one who showed him upstairs didn't look like a whore.

105

'Do you want to stop?' he asked, and the eyes that looked back at him were wary.

'I suppose I do. I know it could kill me in time, but when I go without it, even for a day, I feel as if I'm going mad. My skin itches, I can't sit still, I want to shout and fight everyone. I can't do anything – even dress myself properly. So I take some more and buckle back down to business.'

'You'll have to go away for a complete cure,' he told her.

'Where to?'

'To the country – I know a place called the Moat House at Swanley in Kent. It's very discreet. You can take a companion if you like.'

'Companion? I'm not married and I have no companion.'

'What about the lady who met me when I arrived.'

'That's my business partner, Rosabelle Scott. We're dressmakers. She can't go away because we have a business to run – or you won't get your fee. Can't I break the opium habit at home?'

'You must go away if you want to rid yourself of this addiction.'

'And are you sure seclusion in Kent will work? How would they treat me?'

'You'll be given hot baths, massages and a special diet but you'll not be a prisoner. You can go out for walks and drives, but you must always have someone with you. There will be withdrawal symptoms at first – perhaps for quite a while – but you'll be cured in the end if that's what you really want.'

'And for this advice you're going to charge me ten guineas!' she said and laughed, showing him that she had once been a beautiful and fascinating woman.

When Rosabelle was sent for and told the diagnosis, she looked at Rachelle questioningly and was told, 'I don't want to go away. You're making a fuss about nothing. I can cure myself at home.'

Dr Worthing clicked his tongue and said, 'Far from it.'

'Give me time. Let me think about what you've said.'

Rachelle dismissed him, and he made for the door with Rosabelle behind him. She felt that there was little chance of Rachelle doing what she was told.

In the downstairs hall he said to her, 'Don't be talked out of this. Your friend needs treatment. Try to persuade her to go for a cure, and tell her son to stop buying opium for her. He's killing his mother.'

'Her son buys it?' Rosabelle was thunderstruck. On the occasions she'd met Stan, he was always with Eth, and she sometimes wondered if he was mute because he rarely opened his mouth.

'She told me he bought it for her,' said the doctor, putting on his elegant hat and going out into the busy street.

Rosabelle sent a messenger to Eth, who arrived that evening and was button-holed before she went upstairs to see Rachelle.

'Did you know that Stan buys the opium for his mother?' Rosabelle demanded.

'I never guessed! So that's how she's getting it. I've been wondering why he had so much money in his pocket recently, but he's not a lad any more. I can't tell him what to do,' was the reply.

'Someone has to tell him to stop. If she goes on doping she'll die. The doctor who came to see her today said she ought to go away for a cure, but she's not taking him seriously. She thinks she can stay at home and cure herself, but he says that's not possible.'

Eth pushed past and headed upstairs. 'I'll sort her out,' she snapped.

When she came back again, she told Rosabelle, 'She'll go for the cure. As soon as possible, I'd say from the look of her. Can you go with her?'

'I can't leave the business.'

'In that case, she'll have to go on her own. Get in touch with that doctor to arrange everything before she changes her mind again.'

The organizing did not take long. Three days later, a shaking, shuddering, sweating Rachelle was helped into the doctor's large barouche with Rosabelle, who was going along to see her settled in her place of seclusion deep in the Kent countryside.

Dr Worthing travelled with them in case his patient tried to escape en route. He had seen enough drug-deprived people to realize that their strength could be phenomenal, and Rosabelle, though she was young and strong, would not be able to control Rachelle on her own.

The Moat House was a large and imposing Tudor building, set back behind a vast lawn and a stone terrace where people sat on long chairs sunning themselves.

'You'll be very comfortable here,' the doctor assured his patient as the carriage wheels crunched through deep gravel in front of the entrance. She said nothing, only sat immobile with her black outlined eyes staring ahead as if she was in a trance, but very slowly, enormous tears sneaked down her powdered cheeks, leaving pathetic tracks on the surface of her skin.

Waiting to receive the new patient was a female nurse who looked like a bare-knuckle boxer in a stiffly starched uniform. Her name, she said, was Sally.

'Come on now, madam,' she said to Rachelle, 'I'll get you undressed and into bed.'

For a moment the patient considered rebelling, but Sally's lowered brow and brawny arms changed her mind. As she was led away, she looked over her shoulder at Rosabelle and pleaded, 'Don't leave me here. Take me home.'

Sally looked back too. 'I think it would be better if you left now,' she said.

Returning to London in the barouche, Rosabelle was miserable. She and Rachelle had been together for a long time, though they had never really formed a close friendship like the one she had with Jessie, but they depended on each other, and the life that she had made for herself was due to Rachelle, who took her out of Eyemouth and into a different world.

She said nothing of what was going through her mind to the doctor, who sat beside her, tactfully silent.

'They won't be cruel to her, will they?' she asked eventually.

'Of course not.' When he turned his head towards her, she saw that his eyes were a strange amber colour, like the eyes of a cat. The way he stared made her uncomfortable. It was as if he was trying to read her mind and she hardened herself against him.

'Have you been friends for a long time?' he asked.

'About seventeen years. I've lost count.'

'Did you meet in France?' He was curious.

'Goodness me, no. We met in Berwick-upon-Tweed, if you've ever heard of it.'

'I have. It's on the border between England and Scotland, isn't it? Is that where you come from?'

'No. I come from a fishing port called Eyemouth in Berwickshire . . .' She was at a loss to understand why she was so forthcoming with this man. Had he really hypnotized her? Or was it his professional manner that was drawing her out?

His eyebrows rose. 'Eyemouth! That was where the fishing disaster happened some years ago, wasn't it? I read about it in *The Times*. The Lord Mayor of London launched a relief fund, as I remember. I hope it helped.'

She half turned in her seat and stared straight at him. 'It was handed out, very grudgingly, by churchmen and bigots.'

'How do you know?'

'Because I got some of it – five shillings a week for myself and half a crown for my baby son.'

He was silenced for a few moments before he said, 'I'm very sorry. I had no idea . . . Please forgive me for being crass.'

'You're not crass. You didn't know. Why should you? I was a fisherman's widow. I'd been married for exactly one week.'

He ran a hand down over his face and said, 'That's awful.'

'It was,' she agreed.

'What brought you to Mayfair?' he asked next.

109

'Rachelle did. I went to work for Berwick dressmakers and she was one of their customers. She liked my work and brought me to London with her. We set up our own business, and have done very well.'

'And your son?'

She looked away, staring out of the window at the soft landscape that was so different to her native land. 'My son is still in Eyemouth with his grandmother,' she said stonily.

The giving of confidences was at an end. She did not want to start talking about Aaron.

Eleven

'Who would have thought it?' Gossiping women stared in disbelief at Jessie as, after only two weeks of mourning, she walked down the hill from her big house to the grocery store which she now owned.

She heard what they said and, though the old Jessie would have whirled round and cursed them roundly, she kept a calm expression and stared straight ahead, but inside she was singing her secret thoughts to a little jig tune . . . *No more poverty, no more mussel-gathering. My girls will never have to bait hooks or gut fish on any pier side. Hooray, hooray, hooray!*

She maintained her dignity till she pulled on the elegantly curved brass handle of *her* shop's front door, but then she turned and made a rude derisory gesture, with two fingers stuck up into the air, at the women staring after her.

'*Whoops!*' she cried aloud as she kicked up her heels and disappeared inside.

During the morning, a procession of people arrived, all eager to speak to her. She was especially gracious to Mrs Lyall, who had disdained her in the past, but was now positively fawning. When Alan Cochrane appeared, all Jessie's false front disappeared and her face came alive with pleasure as she ran round the counter to give him a hug that brought a flush to his cheeks.

'I want you to come to supper tonight,' she cried in a loud voice, but added in a whisper, 'and I'll open a bottle of champagne.'

The idea of entertaining in her new house appealed to her

so much that she sent the shop's messenger boy to Effie to invite her and Aaron to the party as well.

The reply came back by return in a short and curt handwritten note, though Effie knew very well that Jessie couldn't read.

It said, 'I can't come to supper. I'm too busy. Mrs Effie Maltman.'

Fanny, who had left her abusive husband and moved back to live with Jessie, was fetched out of the office to read this missive to her sister.

'*Mrs Effie Maltman*! What is she playing at? Are you sure that's what it says?' asked Jessie, peering over her sister's shoulder at the scrap of paper.

'Of course I'm sure. She's signed her name as if it was a legal document or something,' said the indignant Fanny.

'And she's too busy to come to my party? Doing what?' demanded Jessie.

Fanny snapped, 'She doesn't say, but it's obvious she doesn't want to see you.'

'Are you sure?' Jessie couldn't believe it.

Furious, Fanny threw down the paper. It irked her to have to earn her keep as her sister's secretary. 'If you don't believe me, you'll have to learn to read your own letters, or else ask Effie to her face why she's turning down your invitation. Go and ask her.'

Just as angry, Jessie jumped up, grabbed her new paisley shawl and hurried off through familiar alleys to the fisher folks' houses where she had grown up.

As she expected, Effie was at home, mending one of Aaron's shirts, and she burst through the door without knocking.

'Why won't you come to my supper party?' she demanded without preamble.

Effie looked up, grim faced. 'Because I'm mad at you.'

'What about?'

'For not telling me that Robert Stanhope was Poppy's father. You know damned well I asked you often enough.'

Jessie, slightly deflated, leaned against the stone sink and replied, 'Maybe that's why I didn't tell you.'

'What do you mean?'

'Because you kept asking. You worried away at me like a dog.'

'You were playing games with me then?'

'No, I meant to tell you eventually, and I would have, but it was nice to have a secret. Everybody was bursting with curiosity and only I knew the truth . . . I liked that. I didn't expect him to die suddenly like he did, and I was so shocked I let it slip out to you.'

'Some time to tell me, over his dead body!' Effie bit off her sewing cotton with her teeth as if she would rather take a snap at Jessie.

'Aw, Effie, he and I made a bargain not to tell anybody. Getting married was our business,' said Jessie in a more mollifying tone.

'So he didna' want folk to know either. Was he ashamed of you?'

Jessie's face hardened again. 'I was the one who wanted to keep it quiet, not him.'

'Huh, so you'd rather let people think your daughter was a tinker's bastard or something?' said Effie scathingly. They were having a real row now.

With an effort, quick-tempered Jessie controlled herself. '*I* know she's not a bastard. *He* knew she isn't a bastard. He went to his lawyer and signed a paper acknowledging her as his, and the people who knew kept the secret because we wanted it that way.'

'Was it you that was ashamed then? Were you scared folk would say you married him for his money? Because that's what they think.'

A vermilion tide flooded Jessie's cheeks. 'Is that what they're saying? Well, it's not true either. When he first started giving me presents, I enjoyed it, but when I really got to know him, it was different. He was a good, kind man, and he was very lonely. I was the one who changed. I enjoyed comforting him and giving him pleasure the only way I know. Listen, Effie, listen to what I'm saying. I only got into bed with him because I wanted to, and not for what I could get out of it.'

Effie's rage was mollified by Jessie's evident sincerity. One part of her wanted to jump up and embrace the lassie, but another part still rankled with resentment at not being allowed to share the secret of Poppy's parentage. It was hard to accept that something so important was withheld from her.

'You're too easy with your favours,' she said, but the tone was slightly softer, and Jessie seized the opportunity.

With a little smile showing in the corners of her lips, she said, 'I'm not all that easy. There's a lot more ask than ever get. I pick and choose.'

Effie stood up to put her sewing away. 'When did you decide to get married?'

'When I found out I was carrying. I thought we'd taken care, but when it happened . . . he was delighted.'

'How did he know the baby was his?' asked Effie bluntly.

Anger showed again in Jessie's face. 'He knew and I knew. Surely you don't think I'd push another man's bairn on him? Anyway, he was the only one I slept with that summer. It wouldn't have mattered to me if we didn't marry, but it mattered to him. He was worried that when he died, we wouldn't be looked after. Even if he left the baby a legacy in his will, he was afraid Hester would try to over-turn it. But he said that if he and I were man and wife, she couldn't. He was fair taken up with being a father again . . . If you'd only seen him! After she came, I used to take her to visit him and he'd hold her, curling her little fingers round his . . .' Her voice cracked, and Effie's anger seeped away a little more.

'So what happened? Why did you agree to the marriage?' she asked.

'His heart began giving him trouble before Poppy was born, and he pleaded with me again for the baby's sake, but

I said I wasn't ready to become anybody's wife. I liked being free, so he promised to keep the marriage secret. He said if I found another man I liked better than him, I'd be free to take up with him . . . I didn't want to stop having fun, but I didn't want people to point their fingers at Robert and call him a cuckold. He wasn't a passionate man. He didn't marry me only to go to bed with me. He wanted company when he was lonely, and I made him laugh. The funny thing is, I never found anybody else. I was faithful to him, isn't that strange? Jessie the bad girl, I know what they say. But I've changed, little by little. It just happened, and nobody was more surprised than me . . .' Jessie was pleading with Effie for understanding.

'I can't understand how you managed to marry without anyone knowing,' said Effie, who found it hard to believe that Jessie could keep her secret in a town where prying eyes and listening ears were everywhere.

'We got married at Lamberton Toll on the same day as Mary, after the wedding party left. It was at Lamberton that we'd had our first tryst – on Fanny's wedding day, when I wore my braw hat for the first time. He took me to an inn on Holy Island . . . It was grand.'

Effie was silent, with doubt and distrust still showing in her expression, so Jessie exclaimed, 'Don't look at me like that. I'd no idea he would leave *anything* to me, and certainly not the shop. I honestly didn't. I thought he was only worried about his baby. The will was as big a surprise to me as it was to Hester. He said we should marry for the baby's sake, and I believed him.'

'But couldn't you at least tell me?'

'If I told you, you'd tell Euphen, and she'd tell Alex. It would have got round quick enough. Besides, Robert didn't want Hester to find out before she had to. She'd have hounded the life out of him.'

Effie sighed. 'I've never understood you, Jessie.'

'I'm not complicated. Rosabelle's much more complicated than me. I know what I'm like, and I'm not ashamed to admit it. Please come to *Poppy*'s house and have supper with us all tonight. I love you, and the girls love you. Bring Aaron because we love him too. We're a family, Effie; the storm tied us together, and we've weathered that. Don't let this come between us.'

That did it. Remembering the terrible time when they were brought together by death and disaster, Effie realized that she was being petty, so she opened her arms and held them out to Jessie, who stepped up and hugged her back. The breach between them was healed.

Aaron's face lit up when he was told him about the invitation to Jessie's supper party. Though he had said nothing about it, he'd been very aware that his grandmother was in a bad mood and Jessie was the cause. Now that she seemed sunny again, relief filled him because Jessie and the girls were his family as much as Effie, and he did not want to have to sneak away in order to see them.

They were both dressed in their best and joking with each other when they walked up the hill to Beechwood as the sun was setting.

A maid opened the door to them, and Jessie came rushing up behind her with arms outstretched. 'Come in, come in, my darlings. Alan's here and I've put the champagne on ice.'

It was impossible even for Effie not to enjoy herself when this hostess was set on making her guests have a good time.

Still girlish-looking, with dark curls tumbling round her cheeks and eyes flashing, Jessie popped the first bottle's cork and sent it speeding through the air like a bullet, knocking over, but not breaking, a china figure on its way. Everybody laughed, sipped their wine, and forgot that, as far as convention went, they were in a house of mourning, but Jessie was never going to mourn for long.

It wasn't as if she had no feelings, but, for her, life should be lived at full tilt. Timid Rosabelle could do with some of the same spirit, thought Effie as she sat back and watched. Even when Dan's wife came home from London looking like a fashion plate, she was unsure of herself. It was to be hoped that she was happier now, but her letters were still very guarded so it was hard to tell.

They clinked glasses and drank their champagne, not caring that it was wrong to do so at the same time as eating roast duck followed by rich plum cake. Not for them the etiquette that ruled the dinners of their social superiors, though they did use the monogrammed Stanhope silver and ate off fine Doulton dinner plates.

Alan Cochrane forgot his diffidence and surprised them all by making jokes and uncorking a second bottle, firing its cork off in the opposite direction to the first and narrowly missing the chandelier.

Light-headed with champagne, Aaron laughed and looked across the table at Henrietta. At that moment, she raised her head and their eyes locked. To his astonishment, something like an electric shock ran through him. Was it the wine? Was it the laughter? He felt his head swim, but he kept on staring at Henrietta as if he was seeing her for the first time, though he'd known her all his life.

How pretty she is, he thought. How sweetly curved her mouth, how soft-looking her light brown hair, how beautiful her calm, understanding eyes. The way she smiled and nodded her head gently when she saw how he was staring at her was entrancing. He wanted to reach a hand across the table and stroke her cheek, but instead he kept on staring till he saw a blush appearing on her cheeks and then he looked away.

They'd grown up together and she'd always made him feel protective though she was his senior, but by so little that it didn't count. They'd walked to school together; played games on the sand in the same gang of children, shared their dreams and told each other their secrets . . . He could not imagine life without her.

Suddenly he stood up and said, 'I've eaten too much. Come and take a turn in the garden with me, Henrietta.'

Effie looked at him in surprise. 'It's nearly dark,' she protested.

'Not yet, and I only want to walk round the lawn to get my second wind for more champagne,' he said, throwing down his napkin and holding out his hand to Henrietta, who laughed and stood up too as if she'd been hoping for the invitation.

Jessie said, 'Go on. When you come back we'll all play cards – and drink more champagne.'

There was a faint chill in the air as they walked down a broad path that ran between carefully tended flower beds, so Aaron took off his jacket, draping it over his companion's shoulders.

'Thank you,' she said softly, looking up at him, and he felt his hands tremble as he touched her.

'If there was anything in the world you wanted, I'd get it for you,' he told her. The words were out before he'd even thought about them.

'Oh, Aaron, so would I for you,' she said and stopped walking.

He reached out and took her cool hands. 'I love you, Henrietta. I realized tonight that I've always loved you, ever since we were babies,' he told her

'And I love you,' she whispered.

'Like a brother?' he queried and she shook her head.

'No, like a man. I don't think there's anyone else in the world as good or clever or handsome as you. I've always thought that. Didn't you know?'

He sighed. 'I must be slow to catch on but I feel the same way. What's happened to us, Henrietta?'

Off the path was a rustic seat beside a thick yew hedge that shielded it from the house, and they sank on to its mossy seat, holding hands and staring at each other. Neither of them spoke, but, very slowly, their heads came together without their eyes leaving each other's faces. Then, finally, their lips met. It was the first romantic kiss for either of them.

Her lips were soft and tasted champagne sweet. He sighed, drew his head slightly back and then kissed her again. She seemed to melt into him, as if that was where she belonged.

When they drew apart at last, he told her, 'I want to marry you.'

'But we're too young. We're only seventeen,' she replied.

'My mother was nineteen when she got married,' he said.

'And mine was eighteen when she had me, but she won't want me to do the same thing. She's always said Poppy and I shouldn't rush into marriage, especially since Aunt Fanny's marriage has been such a disaster.'

He grimaced. 'I think any marriage of Fanny's would run on the rocks. She'd be hard to live with. But we would be perfect together, I'm sure of it.'

She smiled. 'That's true; it's not as if we have to find out about each other. I know more about you than I do about anybody in the world. And I love all of it.'

He slid his arm round her and she put her head on his shoulder. 'There's something about me you don't know,' he told her.

She looked up in surprise and asked, 'What's that?' With a thrill like nothing he'd ever felt before, his skin prickled as her long eyelashes brushed his cheek when she moved her head to look into his face.

'You don't know that I want to go to art school and learn to be a sculptor. Mr Green the schoolmaster thinks I have talent. He wants me to keep on with it.'

'I agree with him. You're a sculptor already. I've never seen anything so clever as your driftwood figures.'

'Do you really like them?' He carved so many that Effie occasionally forgot they were meant to be works of art, and used them to light her fire in the morning.

'I love them. I've kept every one you ever gave me,' said Henrietta simply.

'I'd like to go to college and learn to work in stone as well as wood,' he told her.

'But what about the boat that Effie wants to buy for you?'

'She was talking about buying me a share of the Purves boat but they've decided not to sell – they want to keep it in their own family – so now Effie thinks she'll buy the *Ariel*

Gazelle. William Burgon doesn't want it because it's too old and decrepit for him, so Mam's thinking of having it rebuilt. She wants me to sign on with Alex as a crewman and take it over when he retires, which will be quite soon, I think. But, Henrietta,' he turned to the girl and stared into her eyes to see her reaction, 'I don't want to go to sea. I don't want a boat, not even the *Ariel Gazelle*. I don't want to be a fisherman. I've been wondering how to tell her. I keep trying, but I never get round to it somehow.'

She nodded with sympathy and understanding. 'You poor thing. She'll head you off if she sees that you've something to say that she doesn't want to hear. I love her but she's the strongest-minded woman I ever met in my life.'

'I love her too and I can't bear to disappoint her. She sees me as another Jimmy Dip. I like the sea well enough, but I can't stop thinking of that bit in Mr Cochrane's book about my father drowning on the Hurkars. I'm not a coward, but I want to do something else with my life. My father and mother were only married for one week. When we marry, I want us to be together for years and years . . . till we're old, old people.'

She put her arms round his neck and pulled his face back to hers. 'I want that too. I want it so much. When I think of your mother and mine losing their men the way they did, I don't know how they survived the pain. I'm glad you don't want to go fishing. It would kill me to lose you like that. We'll have to work out some way of telling Effie. If I were you, I'd speak to Alex Burgon first. He's a fair-minded man, and if he thinks you'd be better off as an artist, he'll talk to her for you.'

By now it was quite dark and the lights from the drawing room shone out into the garden like the beam from a lighthouse, so they ran towards it for they'd been out long enough.

Effie was sitting in a chair by the window and when she saw them holding hands, a strange feeling of foreboding filled her but she drove it away. Tonight was not to be wasted with anxieties; tonight was a time for enjoyment.

*   *   *

Though Aaron had left school, he went back whenever he could in the evenings to work with the schoolmaster, Mr Green, a talented amateur artist who had spotted and nurtured the talent of the boy from fisher town.

Effie tolerated this friendship, but showed little interest in the work they did up at the schoolhouse until one day, soon after Jessie's supper party, when Aaron came home bursting with news.

'Listen to this, Mam! Mr Green has sent one of my wood carvings to an exhibition in London,' he said excitedly.

Effie, cooking as usual, looked over her shoulder at him and said casually, 'Oh, very nice.' It was obvious that she did not put the same value on this news as he did.

Disappointed, he sat down at the table and lifted his fork and knife. 'It's a competition he's entered me for. He doesn't think I'll win a prize because artists from all over the country send in carvings and sculpture, but he liked mine and wanted to send it anyway.'

'In that case you won't be disappointed if you don't win,' she said cheerfully, ladling spoonfuls of mashed potatoes on to his plate.

Deflated, he began eating, and she stood watching him with the same devouring love as she had poured out on him since he was a little boy. 'Eat up. You're going to help Alex on the *Ariel Gazelle* tonight, aren't you? He's sailing tomorrow, and taking you with him, he said.'

'Yes, but . . .' Now was the time to speak out, and his resolution grew, strengthening his voice. 'But I've been thinking that I don't really want to work as a fisherman.'

She stared at him in disbelief. 'Is it that Mr Green who's put this into your head? Ever since he came to the school, you've been acting funny.'

'He's got nothing to do with it. It's me. I don't want to spend the rest of my life on a trawler. I want to do something else.'

'But all our family – on both sides – have been fishermen. It's in your blood.'

Her stared back at her. 'I love the sea. I love watching it, I love sailing on it, but there's something else in me and I want to explore that.'

She abruptly sat down facing him. All at once she looked her age. 'What do you want to do instead?' she asked.

'I want to go to art college.'

She groaned as if he'd told her he was going to prison. 'Art college? Where?'

'There's one in Glasgow and one in Edinburgh. Mr Green thinks Glasgow would be best for me.'

She thumped the table with her fist. 'I knew he was behind this. I'm going to have a word with him.'

Aaron's face was set. 'Don't do that,' he said quietly.

She changed instantly and became pleading. 'Oh, Aaron, it's my dream for you to have your own boat. I've been saving the money your mother sends and there's more than enough now. If you sail with Alex for a year and let him teach you what he knows, you could be the youngest skipper in the port. Jimmy Dip would be so proud of you.'

His face was set. 'Jimmy Dip drowned. All the sea gave you back of him was his head. I don't want a death like that. I want to make things, to see things grow under my hand. I want to be a sculptor. Please listen to me. The last thing I want is for us to quarrel, because I love you, but please listen.'

She knew he meant it, and held out a placatory hand to him. 'I'm listening. I'm thinking. I've never been to Glasgow. I can't imagine what it's like. But how can you make money whittling wood? I want you to be a man of substance, a man with standing in his community. You'll never be able to keep a wife by making figures out of driftwood. And, Aaron, you're all I have. I don't want to lose you. If you go to Glasgow, you might never come back!'

He walked round the table and knelt beside her, holding her hand. 'You'll never lose me. I love you. I'll keep coming back to Eyemouth because I want to marry a girl from here and she won't want to leave either.'

Effie looked at him, her eye as sharp as a little bird's. 'Marry? That too? Who is it?'

I've gone so far, I might as well go on, he thought, and took a deep breath. 'I want to marry Henrietta.'

She jumped from her chair, throwing him off, and gave a cry like someone in pain. 'Marry Henrietta! Oh my God! You canna do that. I'd rather you went to Glasgow and learned to carve anything you like,' she cried. The foreboding she'd felt at the dinner party came rushing back into her mind.

He was astonished at this reaction, because he'd hoped to please her. 'Why not? I thought you loved her.'

'I do, I do. She's my granddaughter. I brought her up the same as I brought you up. She's the sweetest lassie ever born – but you and she can't get married. Listen to me, it's not possible. It's not right for either of you.'

'Why not? Tell me why not!' He was angry now.

'Because you and she are *first cousins*. And not only that, her mother and your mother are second cousins, her grandfather and your grandfather were cousins too, four of your great-grandfathers were brothers . . . Do you understand what I'm saying? You'll have funny children, you'll breed halfwits. If you have to marry into Jessie's family, at least choose Poppy because she was fathered by Stanhope and there's little shared blood between you.'

'But there's a lot of marriages in this town between people with family links and not all the bairns are halfwits. You didn't say anything when Jessie and Henry wanted to get married,' he protested.

'I didn't because the link wasn't so strong as it is with you and Henrietta. But, think about it. Folk that marry their blood relations *do* have idiot bairns. Look at Willie Wake – his parents were full cousins. If his son hadn't drowned he'd have gone the same way as his father in time. This town needs strong, intelligent children to bring it back to life after all the good men were lost in the storm. We need good stock, not dafties!' She was distraught.

'You mean we've got to breed for the town, like animals

123

in a farm?' Furious, Aaron threw down his knife and fork and stormed out of the house, unable to trust himself to say any more.

In a rage, he ran to the harbour and jumped on to the deck of Burgon's boat, making it rock violently on the water.

'Steady on,' said Alex. 'You'll swamp us.'

'Sorry, it's just that I'm mad at Mam.'

Alex laughed. 'What's she done to get you riled?'

The boy looked straight at him. 'First of all, she won't listen when I tell her that I don't want to go to sea. Second, she wants me to marry someone she chooses, not someone I want.'

Alex stared back, solemn faced. 'That's a lot to take in, but marrying isn't a big question yet, is it? First things first. Effie wants you to go to sea more than anything in the world.'

'I know. I hate to disappoint her, but I don't want that and it's my life.'

'That's true. What will you do instead?'

'I want to go to art school.'

Another silence, and then, 'That'll be a first for your family – for any family in the town come to that.'

'What do you think?' Aaron asked anxiously, eyeing the craggy old face.

Alex sighed. 'When I was your age I wanted to be a minister, but that was out of the question. My father owned a boat, so I had to take it over. There was never any question. Since then I've been preaching to folk and driving them half daft wi' the fear o' hellfire. I ken what they say about me, but it doesn't matter. If I'd been a regular preacher, I might have got it out of my system by now.'

'What do you mean?'

'I suppose I mean you should follow your dream. I'll have a word with Effie. Keep calm and don't worry.'

It didn't seem fair to add on the problem of Henrietta. One thing at a time, Aaron thought.

That night he went up to Beechwood and found the girl

he loved alone in the library that still smelled of old Stanhope's brandy and cigars.

When she turned and smiled at him, he grabbed her hands and said, 'I'm so much in love with you!'

Her eyes were shining when she looked back at him. She was the loveliest girl he had ever seen. 'And I love you too,' she said.

He folded his arms around her and hugged her tight. 'I wish we could run away together right now but Effie has as good as told me that she doesn't want us to marry.'

She gasped. 'Mam said that? Why? Doesn't she like me? I thought she did.'

'She loves you. She always has – and she loves me too. That's the trouble. It's because we're first cousins. She thinks we'll have idiot children. She's trying to save us from ourselves.'

'But would it matter as long as we have each other?'

'Not to us, maybe, but it would to Effie. She has this wish to carry on Jimmy Dip's bloodline and to breed strong men for the town. She's been telling me that Willie Wake's parents were first cousins – and not only him. There's been lots of others like him apparently – all simpletons.'

'But I love you. I'll never love anyone else the way I love you,' sobbed Henrietta.

He kissed her, held her face between his hands and said fiercely, 'And I love you. There will be a way out of this. Perhaps I can persuade her to forget her fears . . .'

Henrietta shook her head in despair. She knew enough about Effie to realize that mind-changing was not her way, and that Aaron loved his mam too much to go against her. A terrible sense of sorrow filled her, but she said, 'Let's not worry her by insisting on marrying yet. First of all, she must agree to you going to art college.'

On Henrietta's eighteenth birthday Jessie threw a big party at Beechwood, for which she hired a fiddle band and invited all her fisher friends as well as others from the upper town, mixing them together regardless of the social gulf that existed between the two communities.

Thanks to her, people spoke for the first time to others they had seen going around the town for years, but to whom they had never said a word.

Alex, his son and daughter-in-law turned up, all smartly dressed, and when the fiddlers struck up a jig, he solemnly stood up and extended his hand to Effie, who fluttered like a young girl as they took the floor together.

Watching them, Jessie laughed and said, 'There might be a marriage there one day.'

This surprised Aaron, who repeated the words, 'A marriage? My mam and Alex?'

'Why not? She's not sixty yet and he's still spry though he's a few years older. They've been friends for years and they respect each other.'

He nodded in agreement, and a spark of hope rose in him. If Effie and Alex were to marry, there would be one less objection to him getting away from Eyemouth. A major obstacle to his dreams of going to Glasgow was the knowledge that he could not leave Effie on her own. She'd be so lonely.

'Alex is thinking of giving up the fishing soon,' he told Jessie.

'I know. And she's planning to buy you his boat, isn't she?'

He nodded. 'She wants to pay for the *Ariel Gazelle* to be refitted for me but, Jessie, I don't want to go to sea at all. I want to go to art school in Glasgow.'

Jessie stared into his face for a moment before she said, 'I thought something was wrong. Art school won't impress Effie much.'

'I know. It doesn't.'

'Do you want me to say something to her?'

He glowed as he looked at her. 'Would you? Would you really?'

She nodded, 'Let me choose my time though . . .'

*   *   *

Effie sat by the side of the floor after her dance with Alex, and watched the other dancers. Her eyes were fixed on two in particular – Aaron and Henrietta – and she felt a deep disquiet when she saw the way they looked into each other's eyes.

'They are so much in love with each other!' She felt pity for them but her fears for their futures overrode that. It was her responsibility – indeed her duty – to stop it.

At midnight she decided to go home. Eight or nine o'clock was her normal bedtime and she could not believe it when she heard the long-case clock in the hall sounding out twelve.

As she was pulling on her shawl, Alex walked up beside her and said, 'You canna walk through the town in the dark on your own. Take my arm and I'll escort you.'

She laughed. 'I'll be safe enough. All the town villains are here anyway.'

'Let me walk you home,' he persisted. 'There's something I want to talk to you about.'

Without arguing, she took his arm and they headed off into the darkness. As she looked down the hill towards the guttering street lamps of the fishing town, she sighed and said, 'I love this place. I canna imagine anywhere else that I'd want to live.'

He nodded. 'Eyemouth is in our blood, like the sea.'

She sighed. 'That's what I tell Aaron.'

'You know that I'm giving up sailing soon. I'm getting too old for it. It's a young man's game,' he said.

'It's a job for men like my boys and Aaron . . . but he doesn't want to go fishing,' she said sadly.

'Don't blame him for that. He's a fine laddie, one of the best I've ever known. He's a credit to you, but his heart isn't in the sea and it would be wrong to force him. He loves using his hands. Like his mother,' Alex told her.

'But he can use his hands on a boat,' she protested, reluctant to give up her dream.

Alex shook his head. 'Don't pretend. You know what I

mean, Effie. He wants to make things, and go out into the world.'

She spread out her hand as if to grasp the whole town and the sea around it. 'But this *is* our world.'

'It isn't his – and it wasn't Rosabelle's. If you force him to stay you're only being selfish,' Alex said sternly.

The accusation of selfishness stung her and she protested. 'I'm not selfish. I just want him to do what his family have always done . . .'

'Drown?' asked Alex bitterly.

Her face was haggard in the moonlight when she looked at him. 'He has spoken to you about this, hasn't he?'

'Yes, but I saw it before he told me. He works well, but he's not tied to the sea. When he looks out across the water, he doesn't look to the horizon, he looks inland.'

Effie felt as if her world was collapsing round her. 'Did he tell you what he really wants?'

He nodded. 'He wants to go to college – in Glasgow. Instead of buying him my boat, you should pay for him to study art. He wants to be a sculptor.'

She nodded, thinking of the heap of carved figures in her woodshed. 'His mother would like that. She never wanted him to go to sea,' she said softly.

'Don't hold him back,' Alex told her.

As if she was trying to get away from him, she began walking faster downhill and he had to hurry to catch up. 'Wait,' he called. 'There's something else I want to say to you. Though I'm giving up the boat, I'm not completely broken down yet so I would like you to think about marrying me.'

She turned on her heel and stared at him in amazement. 'Us? Get married? What would folk say?'

He shrugged. 'As you know, I've never paid much attention to what folk say about me, and I don't think you have either.'

She was still stunned. 'That's true, but what about Aaron?'

'He could go on living with us, unless you see your way to letting him go to Glasgow.'

This is a funny way to propose to a woman, he thought inwardly, willing her to clear her mind of long held hopes and prejudices.

She walked on slowly without speaking, head bent, but when they reached her door, she looked over her shoulder at him and smiled, 'Well, Mr Burgon, if you and me are thinking of getting married, you'd better get used to making yourself useful. Come in and get the cups out of the press. We'll talk about this over some tea.'

Before his grandmother was up next morning, Aaron went out early to walk the shore in search of driftwood. It was too stormy to sail, so he walked for hours, gathering up his finds, and put them in the woodshed before walking up to Beechwood, where he found Jessie and her daughters gossiping about the party over a late breakfast.

When Jessie and Poppy went off at last, he crossed the floor to sit next to Henrietta and took her hand.

'I'm miserable. I wish we could be openly pledged to each other. I want to tell everybody you're going to marry me, but Effie is as against the idea as ever. She's as good as told me that it's impossible.'

She kissed him, held his face between her hands and said fiercely, 'But I love you. There must be a way out of this.'

They hugged each other tightly, both sunk in despair.

'I'm very pleased!' said Aaron later that afternoon when Effie and Alex broke the news to him that they intended to marry.

'You don't think we're daft old people?' Effie asked anxiously.

He hugged her tight, laughed and joked, 'No. No dafter than usual, anyway.'

She was blushing as she put her hands on his face. 'I love you,' she told him, so he hugged her again before he stood back and looked at the pair of them.

Their hair was grey, their faces lined, but they were both still vigorous and eager to live life to the full. He hoped that when he was their age, he'd feel the same way, but could not help feeling rueful that his grandmother was the one getting married, but she was also the one standing in the way of his wish to marry Henrietta.

Effie went over to the cupboard beside the fire to bring out a half bottle of whisky. 'I think we should have a toast,' she cried.

Even Alex accepted a glass and they faced each other as they drank.

'To your happiness,' said Aaron.

'To your future,' replied Alex.

Effie looked at her grandson over the rim of her glass and said, 'I want another word with you.'

He said, 'Yes?'

'Alex's been talking to me, and he's made me realize that it's wrong for me to make you go to sea. When do art schools begin their terms?'

'The end of summer, I think.'

'Write and get yourself a place in Glasgow, but keep on sailing with Alex till the summer's over, then he'll retire and you can go to college.'

As soon as he could, he ran back to Beechwood to break the news. Jessie clapped her hands in glee when she heard that Alex and Effie were to marry, and everyone was pleased by Effie's backtracking about art school.

'Has Mam really given up insisting that you go to sea?' Henrietta asked as soon as they made their escape from the house.

'Alex talked her round. He's a fair-minded man.'

'When will you go?' she asked.

'At the beginning of October, I think.'

'How long will you be away?' she whispered.

'Mr Green says the course should last about three years. But I'll come home at holiday times and work on the boats.'

'That'll please Mam. Has she changed her mind about us too?' asked Henrietta.

He shook his head. 'One thing at a time. I can't rush her.

130

She's done so much by backing down over the boat.'

'I love you so much. I wish it was us getting married,' sighed the girl, and he put his arms around her, pulling her towards him.

'And I love you and I wish the same thing.'

Henrietta's eyes were full of tears. 'It's so unfair. We can't help being cousins. It's not our fault. I'll never love anyone the way I love you. I'm sure our children would be all right. My mother doesn't seem very bothered about it.'

'Have you told her we want to get married?' Aaron asked.

'Not yet, but she's sharp-eyed and misses nothing. I'm sure she knows because she and Poppy tease me about you all the time. If Mother didn't approve, she'd have stopped us walking out together long ago.'

Aaron groaned. 'Even if I have to wait till I'm Alex's age, I'm going to marry you.'

She grimaced. 'If it takes as long as that there won't be any reason to worry about children, will there?'

They held hands and stared out across the water until the sun dropped below the horizon and evening crept in. Before they parted, they kissed yearningly in an arbour at the corner of the garden.

With the feeling of his mouth still on hers, she went into the drawing room where her mother and sister were playing cards.

'Isn't that good news about Effie and Alex?' said Jessie, slapping her last card down on the table and scooping up Poppy's trick.

'You cheated!' cried Poppy, but Jessie, unrepentant, shuffled the pack, and started laughing. But her laughter stopped when she realized that her elder daughter was weeping.

'My goodness! What's the matter with you? Are you upset that your mam's getting married?' cried Jessie.

'Oh no, I'm glad. It's not that, it's just . . .' Henrietta put her hands over her face and ran out of the room.

Jessie jumped up, suddenly alarmed by the idea that Aaron might not be as trustworthy as he seemed. Had he made her daughter pregnant? Almost overturning the card table, she bustled after Henrietta, who had taken refuge in the library, and confronted her. 'What's going on? You're not having a bairn, are you?' she demanded to know.

She wanted a grand wedding for her darling child, not a hurried affair with the bride sporting a big belly.

Henrietta looked up in amazement. 'Of course not!'

'Then why are you crying?'

'Because Aaron's going away and I love him so much.'

Jessie let out a gasp of relief. 'Is that all? He's only going to Glasgow, isn't he? He'll be back. You're both young. Eighteen's too early to get married anyway.'

'But he'll meet so many good-looking, clever girls in Glasgow. He'll stop loving me because I'll seem ordinary compared to them.'

Jessie put her hands on her daughter's chin and raised her face up. 'Listen to me,' she said sharply. 'You're not just a pretty girl. You're a *beauty* and there's not many of them around. And it's not because of the way you look that he loves you. It's because of the way you are. He'll be a lucky man to get you. Why don't you get promised to each other?'

'Because we can't do that either. Effie's dead against us getting married, and he doesn't want to upset her. He says she's given up so much for him already – bringing him up on her own and changing her mind about the boat.' Henrietta was crying again.

'What do you mean? Does Effie Young think you're not good enough for Aaron Maltman?' Jessie was furious.

'No, no, it's not that. It's because we're first cousins. She says we're too close in blood! She's afraid we'll have idiot children. She doesn't want that for either of us.'

Jessie jumped up from her chair and walked agitatedly to and fro across the Axminster carpet saying, 'Damn, damn, that's just the sort of thing she would get into her head. She's aye talking about the town coming back to life and needing good men. I'll go down there and have a word with her.'

'Please don't make trouble. Don't upset Mam,' pleaded

Henrietta, but her mother only waved the protests away.

'I won't upset her at all,' she promised.

She waited by the harbour wall till she saw Alex going out with a bucket and mop to wash down the decks of his boat before she knocked on Effie's door, then pushed her way in without waiting for an invitation.

'Sit yourself down, Effie Young, I have something serious to say to you,' she hissed.

'What on earth's wrong? Is it because I'm getting married again?' asked Effie, collapsing into the big chair, taken aback by her visitor's set face.

'No, I'm glad about your wedding. It's about your Aaron and my Henrietta. I hear you don't want him to marry her.'

'It's not that I disapprove of your daughter. She's a lovely girl. It'll be a lucky man who gets her,' said Effie in a conciliatory tone.

Jessie crossed her arms. 'So it's not me or my family that you're against?'

'Of course not! It's because they're first cousins. If he wanted to marry your Poppy, I'd be over the moon with delight. But first cousins marrying! You know what that means, especially in this town where everybody shares ancestors anyway. I want Aaron to have strong, clever children.'

'And I want the same for my girl. You're barking up the wrong tree, Effie. I never wanted to tell you this because you've been a good friend to me, but Henrietta is not your Henry's bairn.'

Effie gasped and her face went white. 'I had my doubts about that in the beginning, but I thought I was only being suspicious. Who was her father?' she asked at last.

'A handsome lad who used to drive the miller's cart. I don't even remember his name. He went off to America before I knew I was carrying. I didn't care. I'd only given myself to him once and it wasn't serious. It was one of those summer things.' As usual Jessie was unapologetic.

'Did Henry know?' Effie asked in a steely voice.

'Yes. I told him, and he said it didn't matter. We were

head over heels about each other by the time I found out. I'd had my eye on Henry for a while, and when the carter's lad went off, he moved in on me. It was wonderful. I really fell in love with him.'

Effie shook her head. 'You were a wild lassie. You still are, come to that.'

'No, I'm not, but I'm not sorry about what happened in the past. I loved Henry and he loved me. I told him no lies. If he'd lived, I'd have been a good wife to him and given him other bairns. But I'm not going to let a mistake spoil my girl's life. She loves Aaron and he loves her.'

'Have you told her?' asked Effie, but Jessie shook her head.

'Not yet, but if you want to, that's all right. It doesn't matter any more. Don't hold this against me, please. I let you think it was Henry's bairn because I admired you so much. My mother was useless and I wanted to belong to your family, so I said my baby was your son's.'

Effie's stern face softened. 'I'm glad you joined my family. You've been a good daughter to me,' she said and hugged Jessie.

'Anderson the relief man was probably the only person I really deceived but I needed his seven and sixpence a week.' Jessie laughed and Effie, to her own surprise, managed to raise a smile too. She knew she was hearing the truth, and, in a way, was not surprised.

'I won't tell them. I'll just say I've changed my mind and their babies'll be fine because we're from good blood lines. Whatever are you going to do next, Jessie?' she asked in mock despair.

'Maybe marry the minister,' was the blithe reply. Effie stared at her in disquiet, wondering if she was making another of her jokes. You never knew with Jessie. At supper that night, when Alex and Aaron came back from the boat, Effie managed to sound casual as she said, 'I've been thinking. Maybe first cousins marrying isn't so bad after all. I've just heard of a couple in Cove who have five fine children and they're first cousins.'

The boy turned and stared at her with a question in his eyes, so she nodded and said, 'If you really want to marry Henrietta, I won't object.'

In delight he swept her off her feet and whirled her round the room.

Next day he went to Berwick and bought a gold ring set with a heart-shaped sapphire and that evening, as he and Henrietta walked to the end of the pier, he suddenly held on to her arm and said, 'Look what I've found in my pocket.'

The hand he held out to her and closed and she looked down at it curiously. 'What is it?'

'Open my fist and find out.'

One by one she uncurled his fingers. The pretty ring lay glittering in his palm.

'It's a pledging ring and it's for you,' he whispered. Starry-eyed she held out her hand and let him slip it on to her finger. 'It's to show that you belong to me,' he told her.

Twelve

'How's my sister?' Eth stood in the middle of the salon with her hands on her hips as if she suspected Rosabelle of having secreted Rachelle somewhere on the premises.

'I don't know. The rules of Moat House say that patients must spend at least two months in total seclusion,' she said.

'Haven't you seen that doctor again?'

'Not since he took her to Kent.'

'Well, I'm going to see him, and ask for permission for someone to visit her. It's been nearly two months since she went there, hasn't it?'

'Tomorrow it will be eight weeks,' Rosabelle agreed, and Eth went away.

Four days later, Dr Worthing turned up at Half Moon Street to say, 'I'm driving to Kent tomorrow. Would you like to go and see your friend? She had a visit from her sister two days ago and coped very well.'

'Is she allowed so many visitors?'

'Yes, the staff are pleased with her progress – but though she's much better, she's not completely out of the woods yet. I know she'd appreciate a visit from you. I'm going down to Kent myself and could take you with me if you want to go,' he said.

His invitation was accepted, and the drive into Kent was pleasant, along pretty roads lined by hop fields and fruit trees. Conversation was strained, however, and as Rosabelle sat back in the deeply upholstered seat of the carriage, she had plenty of time to think. Such a luxurious equipage would cost a great deal of money, she decided.

Dr Worthing was obviously very prosperous, and must have enriched himself by looking after the rich and spoiled. There were, however, many people in London who needed medical attention but had no money to pay for it. She remembered kind Dr Wilkie who never took fees from the poorest people of Eyemouth, and felt a pang of homesickness at the memory, which surprised her.

As Moat House came into view, she asked her silent companion, 'What sort of people are treated here? Are they all like Rachelle? Have they all been overdosing on laudanum?'

'Not at all. There are many different reasons why people . . .' he began, but at that moment the coachman began drawing on the reins of the pair of matched bay horses and it was time to alight.

Rachelle was in her room, staring out of the window. When she turned to look at her visitor, Rosabelle's heart gave a terrible lurch because her business partner had turned into an old woman, skeletally thin, worn-looking and witch-like.

She managed to conceal her shock and they bussed each other, Continental style, on both cheeks, before sitting down side by side on a sofa. It was difficult to find anything to say because Rachelle did all the talking and seemed determined not to admit that she was in a place of detention. The French accent was back in full flow and she chattered brightly about musical evenings and the people she met in Moat House as if she were attending a gigantic house party.

Several of her fellow inmates had titles, which pleased her greatly, and she littered her chat with references to Lord so-and-so, Lady the other, admirals and colonels, honourables and baronets.

'I've been passing out our cards to the women,' she said. 'Many of them will come to us to refresh their wardrobes when they leave here.' This was her first and only reference to the business, but that was what Rosabelle most wanted to discuss.

'Yes, I want to talk to you about the salon. Orders have dropped off terribly. I think we'll have to close down if it doesn't get better,' she rushed out.

Rachelle waved that away. 'Nonsense. You're such a worrier! When I get back everything will pick up. They miss me. That's why they're not coming.'

'But we've very little money in the business bank account and your fees here are heavy.'

'There you go again, looking on the black side. I'll sort it all out soon.'

It was impossible to make her talk seriously and Rosabelle was not allowed to stay long. They parted on stiff terms, with nothing resolved.

On the return journey, Dr Worthing spoke first. 'How did you find your friend?' he asked, eyeing her shrewdly so she knew not to equivocate.

'She looks very ill – very old . . .'

'It is hard to break the opium habit, especially when you don't really want to,' he said.

'Do you mean she hasn't come to grips with it yet?' she asked.

He shrugged. 'At first she was very unresponsive but the staff think she's trying harder now. She still has very bad mood swings and fits of rage though. One day she's as sweet as sugar, the next she's a tiger. They haven't been able to cut off the opium completely yet.'

'You mean she's still addicted?' Rosabelle was horrified.

'It can only be withdrawn little by little. She's taking longer than most.'

'But it's so expensive to keep her there. How do I know the treatment is not being dragged out deliberately?' she challenged.

He looked downcast. 'Don't you trust me?' he asked.

'I don't know you,' she said bleakly.

'I promise you that your friend will be released as soon as possible, but if she was to leave now, she would be back doping heavily again within a week.'

'You seem to have a lot of experience in cases like hers. How much longer do you think she needs to stay?' Rosabelle asked.

He sighed. 'At least two more months I suspect.'

She felt sick. Their funds would barely support such an extended period of treatment, but if she took Rachelle away now, what would happen? The problem needed to be talked over with Daisy and Eth. Meanwhile this journey must be endured.

She sat silently thinking. Was he cheating them? Was he only a mountebank?

She remembered Rachelle's chatter about her well-connected fellow patients. Were they all being fleeced?

'You never told me what sort of people are treated at the Moat House. Are they all rich and addicted to drugs?' she asked.

He shook his head. 'No, some are dying, or are seriously ill with progressive diseases. A few people are out of their minds, and several have alcohol problems. It's not just opium. You are not being cheated, Mrs Scott. Of course you are free to take your friend home at any time, but Moat House is a reputable establishment. Can I tell you something? My own wife was in there for three years.'

Startled, she stared at him. 'Your wife? Is she still there?'

He shook his head. 'No.'

'What was wrong with her?'

'She became mentally disturbed.'

'Was she cured?'

'No, she died two years ago, I'm afraid.'

'I'm sorry. How old was she?' Rosabelle asked.

'Thirty-four.' His voice was clipped.

'That's very young to die.'

'She killed herself. Slashed her wrists with needlework scissors. In spite of being closely watched, she hid them. She was determined to do it.'

Rosabelle shuddered, remembering her poor mother who was also determined to die.

'I'm sorry. It's my turn to apologize for being crass,' she said. It would be insensitive to ask more and they passed the rest of the journey mainly in silence, broken only by short comments on the scenery or the state of the weather.

Then they parted stiffly, both thinking that the other did not like them.

When Rosabelle talked to Eth, it was decided that another visit to Rachelle was necessary and Eth would do it. When she returned, she told Rosabelle, 'I've been at that place again and she's a lot better – nearly cured, I'd say. The shaking's stopped and so have the tempers. Sally, the woman in charge of her, says she might be able to come home sooner than that doctor says. She wants to leave herself because she's worried about money too. She knows the business isn't doing well and that bothers her.'

Rosabelle, busy preparing a trousseau for a baronet's daughter, felt a weight lift off her burdened shoulders when she heard this.

'Dr Worthing was exaggerating then! It'll be good to have her back. We need her. I'm no good at dealing with customers. I'm far too shy.'

'I'll send Stan to tell her she can come out then?' asked Eth, and Rosabelle agreed.

For two days she was light-hearted. Rachelle's room was made ready for her and she was expected home that afternoon, so when Dr Worthing appeared at her studio door, Rosabelle was surprised.

'Is Rachelle with you?' she asked and he shook his head. His face was very solemn.

'Mrs Scott, I have some bad news for you,' he said slowly.

She stared back, eyes wide, looking as frightened as a hunted deer. 'What is it?' she asked.

He was blunt. 'I'm sorry to tell you that Madame Rachelle killed herself last night. I received a telegram early this morning and have just come back from Moat House.'

A rush of fury filled her and she shouted, 'So I was right! What sort of place is that Moat House? Your wife died there and now Rachelle! Why do you go on sending patients to a place like that? How could the staff let her kill herself? Was it scissors again?'

He stoically withstood her anger, staring at her without expression before he said, 'She took a massive overdose of opium and died of a heart attack because of it.'

'An overdose of opium? Where did she get it? She was guarded day and night, wasn't she?'

'Her son visited the previous day. I can't prove it, but I'm sure he gave it to her. She hid it, and took it all last night. I think she meant to kill herself.'

Stan! Rosabelle knew in her heart that it was him who'd given Rachelle the drug.

She pulled urgently on the bell pull and told the maid to send a message to Whitechapel saying that Rachelle was dead and Eth was to come to Half Moon Street at once.

Rachelle's whole family turned up en masse. Rosabelle, in a raging fury, met them in the hall and pointed a finger at Stan.

'You did it. You took the opium to her, didn't you?' she demanded.

He hung his head and mumbled, 'I dunno what you mean . . .'

'Oh yes you do. She died of an opium overdose and you got it for her.'

He began sobbing and fought off Eth, who was batting him round the head with her clenched fists. 'Stupid bastard, you stupid bastard!' she shouted. Cowering with his arms over his head, he admitted that he was guilty.

'The first time I went to see her, she asked me to get her some. Just a little, she said. She was having a hard time in that place without it. I bought some and then she asked for more so she could pull herself together for coming out. I got eight ounces and took it down to her. I put it into her reticule. She was ever so pleased. She kissed me . . .'

Everyone stared at the sobbing man. Not knowing what to do or what to say, Rosabelle turned and climbed back upstairs, leaving them to it.

Daisy arranged a memorial service for Rachelle de Roquefort at St James in Piccadilly which was attended by a large number of fashionably dressed clients and friends of the deceased. After it was over, the body was conveyed by hearse to an East End cemetery where it was buried under the name of Sadie Richardson.

Rosabelle did not attend the interment.

After the service in St James, a church she loved, she sat alone in her pew for a long time while Daisy hovered anxiously in the aisle and eventually put a hand on her arm, saying, 'Come home now,' but the answer was a shake of the head.

'Not yet. I've come to a crossroads in my life and I must think. Leave me alone here for a little while. I'll walk back when I'm ready.'

What am I going to do? Where will I go? She did not feel capable of running the business alone – and anyway its financial reserves were all but exhausted by the Moat House fees.

An hour later, with no decisions made, she emerged to find a rain-filled fog drifting along Piccadilly. As she was putting up her umbrella, a hand fell on her arm and a voice said, 'Let me get you a cab.' Dr Worthing was frowning at her. 'I thought you were never going to come out of there,' he said ruefully.

She shook her head. 'I don't need a cab. It's not far and I don't mind walking.'

'But it's raining,' he protested.

She smiled. 'Where I come from this wouldn't be called rain.'

'Then I'll walk with you,' he said firmly, taking the umbrella from her hand and holding it over her head.

When they reached the crossing in front of the portico

leading into the Royal Academy, the street sweeper, who was always on duty there, saluted the doctor, and rushed out to stop the traffic for him.

'And a good day to you, sir,' he said as they crossed to the other side of the road.

Dr Worthing smiled, paused and asked, 'How's your son, Mr Shanks?'

'He's very well again, sir, thanks to you,' was the reply.

'How do you know his son?' Rosabelle asked in surprise as they walked away.

'He was a patient of mine.'

'Surely he couldn't afford your fees?' she said sharply.

'I don't suppose he could, but I run a clinic and dispensary behind my house in Savile Row where I treat all sorts of people – servants, cabbies and street sweepers – in spite of what you think of me.'

She felt shame when she remembered how she'd mentally scorned him for being a money grabber, a man only interested in treating rich drug addicts. He must have picked up her thoughts.

'What was wrong with his son?' she asked in a humbler tone.

'He broke his leg. He was a footman in a big house and footmen have to be able to run about if they want to find work, so it was important for him to get better.'

'Did he?' she asked.

'Yes.'

By this time they were sheltering under the arch that led into the wide piazza in front of the Royal Academy. Every window of the long building facing them across the courtyard was blazing with light.

'Have you ever been in there?' he asked, pointing at it.

'No, what is it?'

'It's the Royal Academy where they hold art exhibitions. There's a display of sculpture on at the moment. I believe it's very good. Would you like to see it? It might take your mind off funerals.'

She was so remorseful at having misjudged him that she agreed to go. 'Yes, I would,' she said to her own surprise.

Many eyes followed them as they walked into the Academy hall. For Rachelle's funeral she had dressed herself carefully in a gown of her own design, in a deep grey colour with a high, tight neck edged by white pie-crust piping and long, close-fitting sleeves. The skirt was swept back into a small bustle and there were three deep, white-edged tucks round the hem. Her golden hair glowed beneath a tiny, forward-tilted hat with a feather pointing up from it. He felt proud to be seen with her.

'The sculpture exhibition is in two rooms on the first floor,' he said, taking her elbow and guiding her up the long flight of stairs.

When Rosabelle turned a corner into the first room she saw a beautiful stone horse rearing up in a corner.

'That's magnificent!' she gasped. Dr Worthing walked over to it and nodded in approval before he said, 'Yes, it is, but here's one I like more. It's won a prize, I see.'

She walked to where he was pointing and saw a chunky-looking family group carved in beautifully weathered wood. It was of a mother holding a baby with a man standing behind them.

The figures were very solid, rounded and tactile, simply asking to be touched. The mother was bare headed, with a long skirt reaching to the ground, and the father was dressed as a fisherman in a rough jersey and high sea boots.

She stopped dead and gave a little gasp. The father was Dan on the last morning she saw him.

Her companion was bending down to read the card on the plinth of the figures. 'It's sold and it's called *My Lost Family*. It cost someone a hundred guineas. The artist knows how to charge. What an odd name,' he said.

'What is it?' Her throat was so dry, she could hardly speak.

'Maltman, Aaron Maltman. My word, he's from your hometown – Eyemouth.'

She gave a terrible gasp and tears began to flow down her

cheeks. He looked at her in consternation. 'Are you all right?' he asked, wondering if she was overcome by a sudden onrush of grief for Rachelle.

Shaking her head, she went on weeping, with her head lowered and her shoulders heaving. He gently took her arm to guide her to one of the long leather-covered banquettes in the middle of the room and she went with him like a lamb.

Aaron Maltman, a sculptor showing at the Royal Academy? Is it my son?

He had to be. The card said he was from Eyemouth, and Maltman was an unusual name. She remembered that, as a small boy, he'd liked making figures out of driftwood gathered from the seashore.

It must have been no accident that she was taken into the Royal Academy that day. Now she had to go back and see her son again.

Still holding her arm, Dr Worthing sat quietly beside her till the first storm of weeping abated, then asked, 'Why did that exhibit upset you so much?'

Her voice was still broken when she replied, 'Because I think it's the work of my son. As you said, Aaron Maltman is an odd name – and it's my son's name. I haven't seen him since he was a little boy. I'd no idea, no idea at all. Oh God, I'm so happy he won't have to go to sea.'

He nodded. 'But why is his surname Maltman and yours is Scott? Have you been married more than once, or did you make up a name for yourself like your friend Rachelle?'

'Neither,' she said shortly.

He went on looking at her with his eyebrows raised, so she explained: 'In the town I come from women don't take their husband's names. I married Dan Maltman but went on calling myself Scott. My mother-in-law Effie Young was married to Jimmy Maltman. My mother Isa Purves was married to Davy Scott, and so on . . .'

'A matriarchy,' he said.

'What's that?'

'A society ruled by women.'

'I suppose it is. It has to be, really. So many men are lost . . .' Her voice trailed off as she remembered the Hurkars and the day she lost Dan. For the first time she realized how much the pain had eased, though she never thought it would.

By now she was calmer because talking helped, and he helped her to her feet. 'Your son is going to make a big name for himself,' he told her.

'Thank you,' she said, but when she stood up her head was swimming. Her companion was watching her carefully, and she shook her head to reassure him. 'I'm all right now. Don't worry.'

'Tell me about it if you like,' he said quietly.

'I feel so guilty that I gave him away,' she said.

'You gave your son away?'

'Yes. His grandmother and I made a pact. It was easier for him if I backed out of the picture. The first time I went back, I upset him so much I made him wet his bed . . .'

Worthing only nodded, unsurprised.

'For a long time I put him out of my mind, but recently he's begun to worry me again – maybe because of Rachelle's Stan, though I wouldn't want a son like him, but when I see women of my age with young men who could be their sons, I envy them.'

He nodded again. 'You're lonely. Have you no other family?'

'A sister in Boston. I haven't seen her for over eighteen years.' Her memory of Clara was of a tall, thin, black-clad figure who'd chivvied her out of her room after Dan's death. It was so long ago.

'You should go back home to see your son, and mend the breach. It sounds to me as if it wasn't entirely your fault.'

'Yes it was. I wasn't very maternal. I never fed him myself. Effie, my mother-in-law, did everything for him.'

'And she took him from you.'

Rosabelle was vehement in Effie's defence. 'He was better off with her than he was with me. He looks so like his father, you see . . . Every time I looked at him, I felt

146

such sorrow. I thought the father had to give up his life to let the son live.'

'That's not logical, or no child would ever have a father.'

She shook her head. 'It's because of the saying – *one goes out when another comes in*. People at home kept repeating it to me.'

'It's nonsense,' said Worthing sharply.

She paused and stared at him. 'You're right. I know that now, but I didn't know it then. I really believed it.'

He held her gently by the elbow as he guided her down the Academy stairs. 'Go back to Eyemouth. Meet your son and your mother-in-law again, re-establish yourself in their lives. I'm sure he'll be glad. Once you've done that, you'll know what you want to do with the rest of your life.'

She stared at him wide-eyed and told him, 'You're a very wise man.'

'It's decision time,' Rosabelle told Daisy next morning.

'And you've decided?'

'Yes, I think I have. I'm going to sell the business. Don't worry, I'll make sure that you're secure because you've been such a support and good friend to me. You've changed my life.'

Daisy looked stricken. 'I'll miss you. You've been my best pupil in every way.'

'We won't lose touch. I'm determined about that. But Rachelle's family are pressing me to give them the money for her share of the business, and I don't want to go on doing this without her. She was exasperating but, in her heyday, she was brilliant. I'm not a businesswoman and don't want to be. What I really want to do now is paint . . . but that's something for the future.'

'You'll be a very good painter,' said Daisy with conviction.

'Before I start painting though, I'm going home to see my family. I might even go to Boston to see my sister. I haven't decided about that yet, but I'm definitely going to Eyemouth.

Now, let's start the process of selling Rosabelle and Rachelle. How do I go about that?'

During the short time it took for the business to be sold, Daisy boosted her confidence, and Dr Worthing was a frequent caller at the house in Half Moon Street.

Money was not an immediate problem because, for many years, while Rachelle spent money lavishly, Rosabelle had been cautious and her bank account was very healthy. As soon as the business was advertised for sale, potential buyers arrived, all trying not to look too eager.

As if the ghost of Rachelle was sitting at her shoulder, Rosabelle stayed cool and fended off low offers till a satisfactory one was made. She was about to accept it, when a rival *modiste* with premises in Mount Street entered the field saying that she would buy the stock, the premises and take on the staff, including Daisy – all for a surprisingly high price.

On the day Rosabelle accepted this she felt as if she'd been reborn and when the contract was signed, she summoned her staff, holding out her hands to them as she said, 'It's done. Your jobs are safe. The woman who is taking over is capable and talented. The business will go from strength to strength. Thank you all so much, so very much!'

And thank you, Rachelle, she thought. Without that strange, masquerading woman, her life would have been so very different. Now she was rich, with enough money to do anything she wanted. *Thank you, Rachelle!*

Unknown to Rosabelle, Daisy sent a message to Dr Worthing to say that the deal had been done, and he turned up that evening to give his congratulations.

'Are you planning to return to Scotland?' he asked.

She had not written to Effie to tell about the upturn in her life or about Rachelle's death. If she went home, she wanted to surprise them. Now she was decided.

'Yes, in three days' time,' she said.

He raised his eyebrows. 'In that case, will you do me the

honour of dining with me the evening before you leave us?'
he asked.

'Dine with you? Where?' She was surprised. No man had
ever asked her that before.

He laughed. 'Anywhere you like, but how about Oscar
Wilde's favourite place, the Café Royal? It's in Piccadilly,
not too far away.'

She laughed too. 'I live my life in a small space, don't I?
Never far from Piccadilly. Yes, I'll dine with you.'

She felt like a girl as she dressed for this last appointment. There was nothing in her normal wardrobe sufficiently smart for the Café Royal, so she decided to wear a
dress that was displayed in the salon as an example of her
work.

It was beautiful, tight-waisted and full-skirted in pale green
voile with a low-cut neck and enormous bunches of frilled
gauze and ribbons on the point of the shoulders. In it she
looked like an exotic butterfly, and when Daisy saw her
coming downstairs, she clapped in enthusiasm.

'What a picture you make!' she cried as she watched the
maid drape a green velvet cloak gently over the huge puffs
of the sleeves.

Though she had been so many years in London, Rosabelle
had never dined in any restaurant, far less one as smart as
the Café Royal, which had gilded carvings on the ceiling
and long mirrors lining the walls. Black-clad waiters flitted
about tables covered with starched white clothes that reached
down to the floor. Elegant glasses glittered by each place
setting; gas lights hissed inside moulded and gilded glass
globes, and potted palms filled every corner.

When her cloak was taken off by an attentive waiter, a
hush fell over the other diners and she flushed in embar-
rassment, but Worthing, seeing her confusion, put a reassuring hand on her elbow and said, 'They're struck dumb
with admiration, my dear.'

Buoyed by his frank appreciation, she glowed.

They talked without stopping as they were served with

dish after dish, though afterwards she was unable to recall exactly what she ate or said. At his insistence, she drank champagne and giggled as the bubbles tickled her nose. It made her forget her crippling shyness and she was able to talk, laugh and even flirt a little, though she didn't know that was what she was doing.

'I know very little about you really. I don't know your first name,' she told him.

He laughed. 'It's James, and before you ask, I'm childless and forty-two years old. I was born in Salisbury where my mother still lives, and I have a brother who is a canon of the cathedral there. My father was a canon too. I studied medicine at Oxford, and when I was twenty-eight I married the daughter of one of my father's colleagues . . . She was twenty-four and her name was Florence.'

'And like Dan, she died,' said Rosabelle in a low voice. She remembered that tragic story from their previous conversation.

He nodded. 'Her family did not tell me – or anyone – that from adolescence she'd been subject to attacks of mania. They hoped she'd grow out of it, but she didn't. It got worse, so bad in fact that she had to be confined in Moat House. She tried to kill one of the maids, then she killed herself.'

'It must have been awful for you,' said Rosabelle, fixing her eyes on his face.

'By the time she died, I was ashamed to realize that all I felt was relief. You have to be realistic about these things. I was left with two feelings – relief and determination that I was not going to marry again, because I thought I must be very bad at choosing a wife,' he said, staring at her with the strange amber eyes that made her think of a leopard.

She faltered and said, 'I'm ashamed to admit that I sometimes wonder too what Dan would have become if he survived. Maybe he'd have taken to drink, like lots of fishermen. And I've almost forgotten what he looked like, though I never thought I would. When I think of him, I see his hands or hear his laugh – but I don't see *him*. It was a shock when I saw that figure my son carved for the exhibition. It brought him back.'

Her companion nodded. 'I remember. He called it *My Lost Family.*'

Her eyes filled with tears. 'He lost his father and he lost me. So you see, I have to go back.'

'Tomorrow,' he said flatly.

'Yes, tomorrow.'

His face was solemn and he said, 'I think we both need a brandy, don't you?'

He showed her how to warm the brandy glass in her hands and breathe in the aroma of the spirit. When she did that, her head swam and she felt happier than she had been for years.

'What magical stuff,' she sighed.

As she sipped it, she remembered the night Jessie brought home a bottle of brandy. 'The only other time I've tasted brandy was when my friend Jessie brought home a bottle that she got from a man who owned our biggest licensed grocery store. She went on to have a baby by him, and they married in secret. When he died, he left her his shop.'

'The young women of Eyemouth sound very formidable,' he said with a laugh.

'Jessie certainly is. I'm looking forward to seeing her again,' said Rosabelle. There were many good things to look forward to when she went back.

Smiling across at her, he thought he had never seen anyone so beautiful.

'I can't bear the thought of you going away and not coming back,' he said suddenly.

She stared at him, the pupils of her eyes enormous. 'I can't come back. I've given up the house,' she said.

'I know. What do you plan to do next?'

'I haven't decided. I might stay in Eyemouth, or go travelling. I'd like to visit France, especially Paris. I used to be terrified by the idea of going on boats – because of Dan dying the way he did – but now I feel brave enough. I hope it's not just this brandy that's giving me courage.'

'I have a better idea. Go home, see your family, and then come back to marry me. I'll take you to Paris.'

They both suddenly went quiet and felt very sober.

She stared at him for what seemed like a long time, before she said, 'Thank you very much. But I have to go home before I can make any decisions.'

'I understand, but I thought I'd better lay my cards on the table before some other man gets the same idea. You see, I'm very much in love with you. I have been ever since we took your friend Rachelle to Moat House. I've never felt like this before,' he told her.

She laid her hand on his and said, 'Thank you very much. I'm very flattered and I promise I'll think about it.'

Thirteen

Effie's letters had been infrequent recently, as if she was too occupied with her own life, and Rosabelle was surprised that there had been no mention of Aaron sending a sculpture to the Royal Academy – but, she realized, that probably would not seem very important to his grandmother. If he brought home a record catch, she'd certainly write about it.

She wanted to surprise them all by turning up unannounced, especially because she was unsure whether she was still held by her promise to leave Aaron alone, in spite of the fact that he was now an adult. The train journey seemed very long and tedious, but after they left Newcastle, she began to gather her possessions and was waiting in the corridor when the train drew into Burnmouth.

The guard who reached up to open her carriage door shouted out, 'Next stop Eyemouth!' and she stood still in astonishment. Leaning down, she asked him, 'Did you say Eyemouth? Is there a station there now?'

He laughed. 'Oh aye, there is, lady. You must have been away a long time.'

I have been away for a very long time, she reflected and sat back in her seat for the time it took to cover the next few miles.

Eyemouth station looked smart and brightly painted when she stepped down from the train. A uniformed porter came hurrying towards her, eager to assist a first-class passenger, and she recognized him as an old schoolfellow.

153

'Hello, Eck,' she said and was disconcerted by the blank look on his face. He had no idea who she was.

'Don't you know me? It's Rosabelle Scott,' she explained, and at last he smiled.

'My gosh, Rosabelle, ye're awfy swell. I wouldnae hae kent ye,' he said.

She knew that in the ten minutes it took to walk to Effie's, the news of her return would be all round the town.

He lifted her bags on to his trolley and asked, 'D'ye want me to send these down to Effie's for you?'

'Yes please,' she told him and he grinned.

'I expect you're back for the wedding then?'

What wedding? But he obviously expected her to know what he was talking about, and it would not do to let him see her ignorance, so she only said, 'I am.'

Walking beside her, pushing the trolley, he was eyeing her with open admiration and curiosity. 'It's marrying time in town right now. It seems everybody's doing it. What about you?' he said with a laugh.

She shook her head with a smile but inside she was wondering if there was a local saying connected with marriages – *one gets married and another breaks up*, or something equally foreboding.

Apart from a new branch railway line and station, the town seemed exactly the same. The day was bright and sunny, making brass handles and fingerplates on shop doorways glitter; the alleys and doorways were carefully swept by house-proud women; and every doorstep gleamed with red polish.

Until Rosabelle went to London, she hadn't appreciated how clean her hometown was – even when at their poorest, women scoured their doorsteps and polished their windows every day.

Even the gulls, perched on roofs and masts, looked well groomed and glossy, not like London's scruffy, scrofulous pigeons. As she walked along, she eagerly looked around but resolutely avoided staring out at the open sea. She was not yet ready to catch sight of the Hurkars.

There was no reply when she knocked on Effie's door, and she stood looking around in confusion. Effie never went very far from home so she'd probably be back soon.

A woman she recognized as one of the Purveses walked by and asked, 'Are you looking for somebody, madam?'

Madam? Here was yet another old acquaintance who didn't know her.

'Yes, I'm looking for Effie.'

'She'll be up at Beechwood making the arrangements. Do you want somebody to take you there?' The questioner's eyes were sharp and curious, and Rosabelle wondered if she had been completely transformed into a complete stranger by her years of absence.

'No, I can find my own way,' she said. What arrangements were being made at Jessie's big house? she wondered.

The Purves woman suddenly gasped. 'I thought I knew your face! It's Rosabelle Scott, isn't it? My word, you've changed. You're quite the lady now.'

Every detail of Rosabelle's smart travelling costume and matching hat were being taken in and memorized for future description.

'Are you back for the wedding?' There was the question again. Whose wedding? But Rosabelle nodded and smiled, hiding her ignorance.

'Of course,' she said.

The big front door at Beechwood stood ajar when she got there. The house seemed to have lost its old stiff formality, thanks to Jessie probably, and Rosabelle stepped into an empty but untidy hall, more and more relishing the idea of catching her family unawares.

She heard voices coming from a drawing room on her right and its door was open too. Peeping in, she saw Jessie, Effie and two young girls sitting at a table covered with bits of paper. Sitting in a chair on the other side of the table was a man she recognized as the Reverend Cochrane. Like the house, he had changed, and looked much more relaxed than he'd ever been before. As she stared at the tableau, she felt her throat tighten and tears welling up in her eyes.

'Hello,' she said in a strangled voice and they all turned to look at her. It was obvious from their expressions that even they, for a few seconds, had no idea who she was. But Jessie was the first to recognize her.

'Heavens above! Rosabelle!' she shrieked and jumped out of her chair, scattering papers as she did so.

Effie followed, arms extended and tears flowing. 'Oh, lassie, how did you know? I wasn't going to tell you till afterwards. I was afraid you'd think I'd gone daft!' She was crying.

They crowded round her, Jessie and Effie almost fighting to hug her first. Laughing and weeping at the same time, she hugged them back. With one holding on to each arm, she was dragged into the drawing room and pushed into a deep sofa.

'Look at you! Just look at her, Alan. Isn't she a swell? My word, what a bonny hat!' Jessie cried.

The minister was blushing, shyness returned, but he nodded and said, 'Very smart,' in agreement with Jessie. It seemed as if he'd never dare to disagree with her about anything.

The young girls turned in their chairs, watching this scene with open curiosity and Rosabelle asked them, 'Are you Henrietta? Are you Jessie's other daughter?'

They nodded, and the younger girl, a replica of her mother, came across holding out her hand, 'Hello. I'm Poppy,' she said.

'I'm Rosabelle.'

'Aaron's mother?' asked Henrietta, jumping up too and rushing across.

'Yes, I'm Aaron's mother.'

'I'm betrothed to Aaron,' the girl said proudly.

'Oh, my dear! Are you the ones who are getting married?' Rosabelle asked in surprise. Surely Effie would have told her about that?

Effie laughed. 'Not yet. In a couple of years, when he's

finished at art college, they'll do it. It's me that's getting married. Can you imagine that? At my age!'

Rosabelle was staggered by this revelation, but she managed to ask, 'Who to?'

Jessie rescued her. 'Isn't it grand? Alex Burgon and Effie are getting married in his chapel the day after tomorrow.' Effie was giggling like a girl, but watching anxiously to see Rosabelle's reaction.

'How did you know to come home for the wedding?' she asked.

Rosabelle flung out her arms and hugged her mother-in-law, saying, 'I don't know myself but I was certain I had to come back. It must be magic. I'm so pleased, so very pleased. Alex's such a good man. The fairies must have told me to come home now.'

Jessie and Effie began arguing noisily about where Rosabelle should sleep. 'There's plenty of room here. I'll put her in the big front bedroom,' Jessie said, but Effie shook her head.

'No, she'll come back home with me. Aaron's back from the fishing tonight and he'll want to see his mother. What a surprise it'll be for him.'

That clinched it, and Rosabelle was relieved because she knew that Jessie's front bedroom had an open view of the sea – and the Hurkars.

Besides, she was desperate to see her son and wondered if he too would not know her.

Aaron was whistling when he came swinging through Effie's front door that evening and stopped in surprise at the sight of three valises standing at the bottom of the stairs.

'What's happening? Are you going someplace?' he called in to Effie, who shook her head.

'No, come in. We've got a visitor.' She pointed to Rosabelle, who was sitting half hidden in the corner of the big fireside. The lamps were deliberately left unlit and he could not see her clearly in the gloom.

Her heart was beating so fast that she felt a pulse throbbing in her neck. *Let him know me, oh let him know me*, she silently prayed.

He stared at her for a moment, and then, thank God, he said only one word, 'Mother.'

She ran across the floor and hugged him tightly, relieved that the likeness to Dan was less striking now. His hair was not as jet black as his father's, and he was leaner too.

'Mother,' he said softly again.

'Son,' she replied, sinking her face into his chest, wetting his shirt with her tears.

'Are you back for the wedding?' he asked, but she shook her head.

'I came back because I saw your carving *My Lost Family* in the Royal Academy. You're very talented, Aaron.'

He beamed. 'You saw it? It won a prize, you know – and somebody bought it.'

'I know. I'm so proud of you.'

Effie's voice came from behind them. 'And here was me thinking you'd come back to dance at my wedding!' But she was smiling when they looked at her.

'I'll do that too,' promised Rosabelle.

Because he was sailing next morning Aaron went to bed before nine o'clock, but Effie and Rosabelle sat on at the fire, staring into its red heart and talking.

'Do you think it's unseemly for me to marry again at my age?' Effie asked.

'No, I think it's a very good thing for both of you. You should have done it long ago,' Rosabelle told her.

'I worried at first in case I was betraying Jimmy Dip, but it's different this time. Alex is my friend, the companion of my old age. Jimmy was my first lover and the father of my children – it's different now; we're different. We're happy. Are you happier now, Rosabelle?'

Rosabelle frowned. 'I don't know. In a way I've come back here to find out. I'm at a crossroads in my life, you see. Rachelle, my partner, recently died and the business has been sold. I've enough money to live without working for the rest of my life, but I don't know where I want to go or what I want to do. I could go to Boston and see Clara. I could travel in Europe like Hester Stanhope. It's confusing having too many possibilities. I'm frightened of choosing the wrong thing.' She did not mention Dr Worthing's proposal.

'At one time I'd have advised you to come home and set up a dressmaking business here, but now that I've seen you again, I know that's not suitable. Strike out, my dear. Be brave,' said Effie.

'That's the trouble. I'm not a very brave person. My instinct is to run for safety and hide.'

'That might have been true at one time but I don't think it is any more. You've grown up more than you realize,' said Effie, rising and pulling Jimmy Dip's fob watch off its place on the mantelpiece. 'It's midnight. We ought to go to bed. There's a lot to be done tomorrow.'

When Rosabelle and Effie arrived at Beechwood in the morning, they found it in turmoil. In the hall Jessie was berating a cowed-looking Mrs Lyall.

'I don't like that gown you've made for Effie. It makes her look fat. I want her to look elegant, like Rosabelle.'

'But she is fat and you ordered a crinoline though I told you they're out of fashion,' protested Mrs Lyall.

'I've changed my mind,' said Jessie grandly.

Lengths of cloth were draped over the chairs of the drawing room, and Rosabelle picked up a soft, pale grey ribbed silk that crumpled satisfyingly in her hand. The longing to create again seized her and an idea for a design leapt immediately into her mind.

'Use this,' she said.

'Isn't it too drab? How about purple? She's the bride after all,' said Jessie.

Rosabelle laughed. 'Are you still fond of purple? The grey will look superb if it's made up properly. Like this . . .' She walked over to Effie, draping the cloth over her shoulders

159

before tucking it in at her waist. 'It should be very plain and simple. The detail will be in the flowers, and the hat – but this time, no stuffed birds. There should be flowers bunched on one side of a high crown and a wide brim. They'll bring out Effie's bonny eyes.'

Jessie clasped her hands. 'Oh lovely, but do we have time?'

'Yes, send to Berwick. Fetch Mrs and Miss Gibson if they're still there. They'll make the hat. Mrs Lyall and I can make the dress,' said Rosabelle.

The next few hours were like being back in Half Moon Street, with Rosabelle making sketches and pinning bits of material together while Mrs Lyall stitched away. Old Mrs Gibson was dead, but her daughter turned up with the perfect hat, and was delighted to see her old employee transformed into a woman of fashion.

At eleven o'clock that night, Rosabelle finally stood up, stretched and said, 'That's it. It's finished. Oh, I'm tired.'

Jessie, looking concerned, said, 'Go to bed. It's all ready and warmed for you. In the back bedroom. I know you don't want to see the harbour . . .'

'No. I won't go to bed yet. The moon's out, isn't it? I think I'll walk down to the sea.'

'The sea? Are you sure?' asked Jessie doubtfully because she knew how much Rosabelle dreaded looking at the Hurkars and the moonlight was bright.

'It's time for me to lay some ghosts,' was Rosabelle's reply.

'I'll come with you,' said Jessie, taking her friend's arm.

A glorious summer moon glowed like a blood orange in the sky and the sea was flat and smooth as velvet. The moon's rays cast a broad path across its surface, as if inviting the watchers to walk along it.

Arm in arm, the two women walked along the harbour wall to the end of the pier, and, bravely, Rosabelle raised her head to stare across the bay at the rocks she so dreaded seeing, the rocks that had haunted her dreams for years.

Jessie felt the tension in her friend's body and clutched her arm tighter. 'Are you all right?' she asked.

Standing stock still Rosabelle continued to stare out without speaking, but at last she said, very softly, 'I'm all right. Thank God, I'm all right. I feel as if different parts of me have come together at last.'

'What do you mean?' asked Jessie.

'It's as if the girl I was before Dan died has found the person I am now. I was wandering in the middle . . .'

Jessie sighed. 'Yes, we all grieved, but you were the worst. You couldn't get to grips with it.'

'Not for a long time. But I'm all right now. I can look at those rocks and feel nothing but sorrow. Before I had such terrible anger . . . and fear. I thought the rocks would get me too.'

'Let's go back. Effie's getting married tomorrow,' said Jessie, gently pulling Rosabelle's arm and leading her away.

Next morning, a glowing Effie with silk roses in her hat and wearing a pale grey gown that made her look like a duchess, stood before the preacher and married her Alex.

The wedding reception was held at Beechwood. During the dancing, Aaron, face flushed, came off the floor, lifted two glasses of champagne and went over to sit beside his mother.

'What are you thinking?' he asked, putting a glass in her hand.

'What do you mean?'

'Begin by telling me all the reasons that brought you back to Eyemouth. You haven't told us everything, have you?'

'No. It was mainly because of your sculpture. It made me feel guilty, so I came back to tell you I'm sorry for being a bad mother. And I came back to find myself and to make up my mind what to do next.'

'You're not a bad mother. You lavished money on me. And you made sure you left me in good hands. Effie loves me and I love her.'

'I know that. In a way I'm jealous of how you and Effie feel about each other, which shows how stupid I am. I'm jealous because you love the woman I gave you to. You're more Effie's boy than mine.'

He took her hand. 'I'm your boy too. After I read Alan's book about the storm, I felt terrible pity for you. You must have almost been driven out of your mind by grief.'

'Yes, I suppose I was deranged for a long time, longer than anyone knew. Till quite recently in fact.'

'What changed you?'

'I had a good friend to talk to and then I met someone . . . I used to think I'd grieve about your father for ever, but that's changed too. I had to come back to make sure, though. I had to look at the Hurkars again.'

He kissed her cheek. 'I love you, Mother,' he said.

When the party broke up Aaron and Henrietta were in the garden, holding hands and staring into each other's eyes. The newly married couple had disappeared, and Poppy was running round the drawing room draining champagne glasses and giggling. Rosabelle left the house to walk to the end of the pier and again deliberately raised her eyes like someone taking a sighting along a rifle, looking out across the sea.

In the gathering evening light, the jagged Hurkars rose from the water. She stared hard at them, challenging them to make her quail and shudder, but they were just rocks, outcrops of stone from the seabed. The terror they once inspired in her had gone. She knew now what she must do.

Next morning she packed her bags at Beechwood before walking down to the fisher town where she found Effie, Alex and Aaron eating breakfast.

'I've come to say goodbye, my dears. I've decided to return to London,' she told them.

'I hope you'll come back for my wedding,' said her son, standing up.

'I certainly will. I might even return before that, and when you're in London to receive more prizes you'll stay with me,' she cried and hugged him tight.

On her way back to say farewell to the people at Beechwood, she stopped at the post office where she wrote out a telegraph message.

It read:

There's an outbreak of wedding fever here and I've caught it stop My answer is yes stop Meet me at King's Cross station eight p.m. tonight stop I'm coming into safe harbour.

Afterword

E yemouth has been a fishing port since the Middle Ages, and today deep-sea fishing is still the industry that maintains the town, though now the boats that sail from its ancient harbour are larger, sleeker and far better equipped than the ones that ventured out on Black Friday, 1881.

The names painted on their prows, however, are still traditional – they are often called after women or flowers – and the men who sail in them bear the same surnames as men who died in the terrible storm.

Shopfronts and tradesmen's vans in the town also carry those surnames, proving that although the men died, their women and children carried on and did not leave. Today people are proud to claim descent from victims of the storm.

People who take their living from the sea always live with uncertainty and Eyemouth is used to sudden, unexpected deaths – though never on the scale of the devastation of 1881. Because of its past, it is not a light-hearted town. A stranger wandering through the narrow streets and alleys that wind between the close-packed houses by the quay will be struck by an indefinable air of sadness and melancholy. Even after a century and a quarter, Eyemouth has not forgotten its dead men. Their ghosts linger on.

In the centre of the town, opposite a red sandstone building with a carved ship above the front door where I imagined Steven Anderson set up his office and handed out the meagre dole to widows and orphans, is the town museum, located in a disused church.

The jewel of the museum's display is a fifteen-foot-long by four-foot-wide tapestry stitched by local women, many of them descendants of the drowned men. It took them two years to complete and is heartbreakingly poignant because they listed every boat that went down, and, beneath it, the names of the men who died. Many of the drowned men were from the same family, and to show kinship, their names have been stitched in the same coloured thread.

The most arresting panel in the tapestry depicts a dismasted fishing boat floating in a still sea with the spread-eagled black figures of seven drowned men floating around it.

This magnificent piece of work was presented to the museum in 1981 to mark the centenary of the tragedy.

The idea of writing about the disaster had been in my mind for some time, and I often talked to local people about their town and their links with the victims of the storm. What finally convinced me to start a book was visiting the museum and seeing the tapestry.

My research came from the newspapers of the time; from *Children of the Sea*, an excellent modern history of the town by Peter Aitchison, himself a descendant of fishermen in Eyemouth; and from *An Old Time Fishing Town – Eyemouth*, a more general history, written in 1901 by Daniel McIver who was a minister of religion in the town at the time of the disaster.

McIver was not a local man but he was fascinated by the fisherfolks' way of life, and he was unusual in being unprejudiced and sympathetic to the plight of the bereaved women and children after the storm. Though he did not actually say so, it is obvious from his book that he felt they received poor treatment from the authorities who disbursed meagre handouts from the vast sum of money sent to the town by well-wishers from all parts of the British Isles.

For my part, I too felt anger at the unfeeling way the families of the dead men were treated – and that was why I found it impossible to look at the tapestry without being

166

deeply affected, for tears were certainly still being shed when it was made.

My indignation and admiration for the people left behind encouraged me to write their story.